THE ROBOT
MEN OF
BUBBLE CITY

By
ROG PHILLIPS

I0616913

ARMCHAIR FICTION
PO Box 4369, Medford, Oregon 97504

*For more information about Armchair Books and products, visit our
website at…*

www.armchairfiction.com

Or email us at…

armchairfiction@yahoo.com

WHAT AWAITS US IN THE DEPTHS OF SPACE?

After fifteen years of space prospecting, Turlogh and Gar were ready to try mining on Pluto, said to be rich in precious radioactives. After landing on the distant planet, they set out to explore its uninhabitable terrain. But soon they came upon something startling. It was an entrance—an entrance obviously constructed by something alien.

A nightmarish adventure then began when they stepped through this mysterious door. Their path followed an underground roadway to a strange domed city, a city whose inhabitants were oddly robotic in nature. Events soon spiraled out of control as they faced imminent danger from this lost race of Plutonians, whose insidious plans reached far beyond the borders of their own frozen world.

FOR A SECOND COMPLETE NOVEL, TURN TO PAGE 107

CAST OF CHARACTERS

TURLOGH HOGAN
He wanted Pluto to be the adventure he had always dreamed of—but what he found was a nightmare world he would never forget.

GAR NICHOLS
After the aliens took most of his brain, he had to learn to live with his 'other' bodies. And controlling them was not an easy task!

FRED GINTHER
After hearing Turlogh's strange tale, this special agent took his investigation deeper and found something decidedly sinister.

GAR HOGAN
He was the Plutonian's version of a human…the difference being he was a robot, controlled by something or someone on Pluto.

VLADIMIR DUBROVSKI
He pressed Congress for a hasty decision—either build bombs and use them quickly, or succumb to an alien invasion!

FRANCES NICHOLS
She took her brothers body back to Pluto for one reason—to recover his stolen brain!

COMMANDER JENSEN
There was nothing like action, atomic bombs, and alien robots to get him in the mood for an interplanetary war!

CHAPTER ONE

TURLOGH Hogan pressed the stud that raised the parabolic projector out of its recess in the hull of his ship. The second the light on the panel flashed on, signaling the projector was in operating position, he flicked the relay button that sent the ultra-high frequency current through its opposing coils.

The wave of nightmare figures that were rushing toward the ship seemed to melt. Their guns exploded, sending fragments of metal in all directions. Then all was quiet.

Slowly a red flag appeared above a large rock. Turlogh frowned. Then he smiled. Red must be the emblem of surrender to these creatures. White was the emblem on Earth.

The scene vanished. Turlogh turned over in his sleep and began to snore gently.

The scene reappeared, but this time instead of waves of the creatures, a battery of high frequency projectors rose above the edge of the gulley two hundred feet away. Turlogh laughed. They were harmless. The hull of his space ship was cushioned from the interior by sound absorbent layers. The ship was designed to nullify the lethal effects of ultra-high frequency.

Again the scene vanished. This time it was gone for some time. Turlogh woke up and listened to the quiet hum of the air conditioner. No other sound was audible. He tried to remember what he had been dreaming about. Finally he gave up. A soft snoring signaled his return to unconsciousness.

Finally the scene came back. This time the most beautiful woman he had ever seen climbed over the edge of the gully and walked slowly toward the ship. In her arms she carried a regulation atom grenade of the type that attaches to the hull and explodes in ten minutes.

He fingered the relay button, and then changed his mind. He could not kill this woman. He pressed another stud that shot anesthetizing gas toward her. She stumbled and fell, and the grenade rolled along the ground, its pin still in place. He watched the gulley, waiting for some other form of attack.

The scene vanished. After a while Turlogh dreamed again. This time he was standing behind a large boulder. He had heard a noise and his new "memory" told him a man was creeping up on him on the other side. A sound as of a pebble moving told him the man was just on the other side of the boulder. Taking a chance, Turlogh jumped out in the open and fired. The bullet caught the man in the chest and he went down.

THE TWIN of the dead man appeared, walking down the path. He was carrying a white flag on a short stick, so Turlogh withheld his fire. When the man came to a stop by his fallen twin he looked at him as if puzzled. Then he asked, "Why did you shoot me?"

"I didn't shoot *you*," Turlogh answered.

"Yes you did," the man insisted. Then pointing at the corpse, "That was me until you killed it, I can't understand. Why do you kill?"

"I kill because I don't want to get killed myself," Turlogh replied.

"Why should that bother you?" asked the man. "Don't you have other bodies?"

Turlogh woke up with a start. The memory of the dream was vague, but the words, "Don't you have other bodies?" were vivid in his memory.

He lay there in the darkness, listening, and trying to recall the dream. The elusive wisps of thought slowly fell into place, until every detail of the dreams returned.

Then he tried to rationalize the dreams, but no scheme he knew of seemed to fit. Possibility of outside origin? He shrugged off the thought, but it returned. The ship was in a closed orbit, circling Pluto and about three hundred miles above its surface. It had been in this closed orbit for three weeks, Earth time, while topographical maps were being made of the surface of Pluto and the planet's solar constants were being measured.

Pluto was rough. With a mean diameter only two hundred miles greater than that of the Earth and a period of rotation only one minute and twenty seconds longer than that of Earth, and acceleration of gravity at the surface almost exactly the same as that of Earth, its mountain ranges dwarfed even the Everests of the home planet. The highest peak so far measured sent its granite spikes sixty-three thousand four hundred and twenty feet above the mean surface.

And in contrast there were tremendous depths that seemed almost bottomless. Great yawning chasms that were miles in depth. No oceans could have ever covered this world or the chasms would have been leveled off, filled with ice.

Solidified gas covered most of the surface to a depth of several feet; but in three areas the rocky surface was free of this covering, and around the edges of these three areas the snowy deposit gave off steamy tendrils that proved the cause of the bareness to be internal heat.

Large deposits of radioactives had been the verdict of the solar survey ship that had first come here in 1987, ten years before. They ought to know since they were equipped to identify any type of radiation.

In fact, that was why Turlogh and his partner, Gar Nichols, had come this far. In fifteen years of space prospecting they had amassed enough wealth to take the big gamble, as they called it. Radioactives were found only on planets of large size. The asteroids had been kind to them, or perhaps the gods of chance. Three million tons of pure copper, a million and a half tons of pure silver, and one fifty ton diamond had been their haul from the asteroids. All had been neatly dropped into the Arizona desert country except the diamond, which they had taken aboard through the cargo hatch and brought down easy.

NOW, WITH fifty billion dollars to their credit in the World Bank, and a new ship around them, they were making a try for the radioactives of Pluto.

Turlogh reviewed all this in his mind as he lay quietly in his bunk. Life on Pluto was impossible, so the dreams could not have had an outside origin. He decided to say nothing to Gar lest his partner think he was getting space wacky.

The alarm clock began to buzz in its niche just over his head. He shut it off and climbed out of the bunk. Today was to be the big day. They had decided to land on a level stretch in the center of the largest warm area. The rocks there were only fifty degrees below zero, Centigrade.

In three more hours the instant would arrive when the landing trajectory would be started. Meanwhile, there was breakfast to occupy the time. Gar was already in the dining compartment, two no. 7 breakfast containers from the cold storage room warming in the heaters designed for them. His huge frame was sprawled out on one of the built in benches, and he was busy rechecking the figures for their landing recoil charges.

He looked up, a friendly smile on his overly wide face, at Turlogh's entrance.

Then, taking in Turlogh's expression, he asked, "What's the matter? You look like you had a tough night."

"I did," Turlogh answered. "Did you have any dreams last night?"

"Not a one," Gar said. "Why? Wait a minute, I'll bet you had some sort of remarkable dream that you can't explain, and you are wondering if I did, too. If I did, then you could explain yours as the result of 'something we ate' no doubt?' Am I right?"

"Partly," Turlogh admitted. He gave a full account of his dreams during the course of the meal. At the end, Gar had to admit that it might be wise to take every precaution after landing. It was just possible that they might be running into something out of the ordinary.

So it was with high pitched excitement that they pressed the stud that released the measured blast from the forward rockets which would slow them down and start the ship on its downward journey.

Strapped in their seats they were safe against sudden velocity changes up to eighty miles an hour. The springs that held these seats were of the ratchet release kind. That is, any sudden compression or stretching of the springs was held by a ratchet mechanism and slowly released by shock absorbers. The chairs were held in suspension in the center of the pilot room, the control panel rigidly connected in front of them.

The landing trajectory was started long before the landing spot could come into view, but when it did come into sight the visual control mechanism could be operated. This was a development based on the same principles as the Norden Bomb Sight. Split images of the landing spot were kept in line in the eyepiece. The automatic mechanism did the rest, bringing the ship to a stop almost without a jar.

The ship came to rest in the center of a table of flat rock that was perhaps a hundred yards wide and twice that long. As the last echo of vibration died to inaudibility the two men unstrapped themselves and climbed out of their seats. Then they went close to the viewports to get their first good look at the surface.

The tableland outside was sharp and jagged. The lava, perhaps millions of years ago, had cooled without the tender care of atmosphere, with its convection currents and constant pressure. Huge lava bubbles had formed, solidified, and broke, leaving almost razor sharp edges of the broken bubbles which gave the whole a chicken wire effect. This was spoiled somewhat by the many fine cracks that spread in all directions, cracks caused by the rapid cooling of the upper few inches of lava while that underneath cooled more slowly.

No erosion had ever been possible. The scene had no doubt remained unchanged for unknown centuries.

TURLOGH looked out the port, his eyes fixed in staring intensity. Gar, turning to his companion to make some casual remark, noticed this and asked, "What's the matter, Turlogh? You look like you've seen a ghost."

"I have," remarked Turlogh. "This is the spot where the ship was in the dream, down to the last detail!"

A grim look appeared on Gar's face. "Then it was no dream," he said. "Suppose there is some super intelligent race on or in this area. We coasted around this planet for three weeks. They would know about it. Now suppose they contacted you mentally and posed several problems to you. In your dream state you would solve them just as you would if they were real. That way they could find out what we have in the way of weapons and also our ways of doing things. Then they would figure out how to take care of us when we land without making any mistakes."

"That's the way I have it figured myself," Turlogh answered slowly. "What'll we do?"

Gar didn't answer at once. Finally he said, "Suppose we just squat here for twenty-four hours and see what happens, all ready to blast off if we have to?"

Turlogh shook his head. "No," he said with a note of finality. "There are only two things to do. We either get away now and report evidence of life on Pluto and try to get an expedition to come here, or we assume that whatever form of civilization probed my mind will be friendly, and go ahead and explore. The last is foolish, but we got rich being foolish, and I am inclined to carry our luck this one last mile."

"So am I," agreed Gar. "Let's go."

The two men donned vacuum suits with oxygen tanks good for twenty-four hours and, with the latest type of sub-machine guns under their arms, stepped onto the planet. Turlogh kept his eyes warily on the lip of the tablerock, but nothing appeared.

Gar's voice came through Turlogh's earphones, "I feel foolish. Here's a planet that could not possibly support life of any kind, and we are acting like we were in the middle of an alien city, expecting some creature that can live in a perfect vacuum to be hiding behind every boulder."

Turlogh chuckled and added, "All on the strength of a dream, too."

The tension somewhat relieved, the two men walked over to the edge of the table and inspected the slope that dropped down at an easy angle for almost a mile, to bring up at the base of a cliff.

The cliff was honeycombed with large openings which might be shallow or deep. It was impossible to tell because the few rays reflected from the surface under direct sunlight into the round openings were not enough to bring out details.

Turlogh, who had been carefully scanning the slope, pointed to a large boulder half way down. "That's the boulder in the dream," he said.

"Well," Gar replied, "we haven't met anything yet. Evidently they have rejected everything they tried in the dream and have something new up their sleeves. Should we go on down?"

Turlogh's answer was to start down the slope. The two men carefully picked their way. One slip and they might puncture their suits, letting the air out. They had each had the space bends in their years of adventure at some time or another, and felt the terrible sensation of the air in their lungs spreading and pushing against their ribs, the prickly feeling of thousands of tiny blood vessels bursting over the skin, and the two to three weeks of constant itching as they healed. Anyone who has experienced this once will forever after go to great lengths to avoid the possibility of it happening again.

CHAPTER TWO

THE TINY SUN, now directly overhead, sent knife sharp pencils of light over the slope. Shadows were black patterns woven into the scenery. Visibility was really worse for details in direct sunlight than it would be later when the starlight would not have to compete with it. After the sun went down the iris would open up full, letting in the faint reflections from cavities in the uneven terrain.

Gar and Turlogh rounded the huge boulder half way down the slope and kept on. After almost an hour of careful stepping they neared the base of the cliff. And directly in front of them was a perfectly round, flat, metallic cover, obviously artificial, held in place by two heavy hinges on the right side and a clamp on the left that was very similar to those which hold cold storage doors in place.

They paused and looked at it. There it was. Set in the face of the cliff, silent, somewhat sinister. The utter silence of space suddenly became a living thing, impressing on them the fact that home was millions of miles away, and that here was the entrance to something alien. Something that knew they were there.

Gar turned and looked up the slope as if estimating their chances of climbing back up unmolested. Then he faced the door once more and spoke into his microphone, "You open the door, Turlogh. I'll be ready to blast anything inside. Stand to one side so that if there is air inside, the door won't hit you."

Turlogh stepped carefully forward and pulled down on the door clamp until it cleared the door. The door remained motionless, so he pulled it open. Inside was a chamber lit by an overhead globe of the cold light variety. Ten feet in was a similar door.

The two men stepped inside and closed the outer door behind them, clamping it shut. Almost instantly their vacuum suits started to collapse as air of some sort began to fill the chamber.

The inner door swung open slowly, revealing a well-lit tube station with one almost conventional looking car standing on the rubbery looking road surface.

"Should we take a chance on the air?" asked Gar.

"I'll do it first," Turlogh replied, taking the front cover off his helmet. He breathed deeply several times and then nodded.

Gar took off his face plate and sampled the air. It had a slight tang to it, evidence of fair ozone content.

"I think we might as well leave our vacuum suits and one of the guns here in the airlock," Turlogh said. "Undoubtedly it's known we are here. We're being handled at the end of a ten foot pole so far. They must think we are as dangerous as a bag full of wild cats or they would have met us up here. If we run into trouble it would be better to have our suits safe."

When the suits and the gun were in the lock, Gar closed the door and started studying its details, hoping to find some way to prevent it from being opened.

Turlogh joined him in the examination. The lever that locked the door in position also closed a valve that let air into the lock. When the door was locked closed a motor started somewhere in the wall, and ran for several minutes. This probably pumped the air out of the lock, back into the cavern, so that little of it would be lost. That which was inevitably lost could be easily replenished by scraping up frozen air from the surface of the planet and bringing it in through the lock.

Gar unhooked the valve lever and hid it on the upper edge of the door. "That ought to do it," he exclaimed with relief. "Now the pressure against the door will keep it closed. Anyone who tries to open it will have to go back and get a new lever arm for the valve unless they think to look above the door."

To prove his point he tried to open the door. It resisted all efforts.

NOW that their suits were safe they turned their attention to the car. Instead of a steering wheel it had a stick, like the stick in a plane. Cautious experiment demonstrated that moving the stick forward caused the wheels to turn to the right, backward caused the wheels to turn to the left, moving the stick to the right caused the car to move forward, and moving it to the left caused the car to back up. The motive force was impossible to determine. The hood was locked. There was no perceptible vibration that might give some hint as to what powered the car.

Finally, with a fatalistic shrug of his shoulders, Gar swung the lever to the right and said, "Well, Turlogh, here we go. If we'll come out, nobody knows."

The roadway spiraled steeply downward, and the car gathered speed quickly, settling at a constant that was regulated by the stick.

Both men kept their eyes fixed on the tunnel ahead, ready for any sudden change in the monotony of the smooth, curving walls. After half an hour the road straightened out and leveled off, Gar slowed the car to a crawl. In the distance could be seen the end where the ribbon of roadway left the tunnel.

"Slow down," muttered Turlogh. "Let's see what we're getting into."

At the mouth of the tunnel they came to a stop and got out of the car. Turlogh kept the sub-machine gun ready for instant use, but as the scene outside the tunnel came into view he dropped it to his side in amazed awe.

As far as the eye could reach spread the fairy towers of a city that beggared description. Buildings so tall they seemed like swaying stems of some giant plant. Spiderwebs of roads that wove in and out among the buildings. And everywhere there was movement as millions of cars and moving figures went about their business, apparently oblivious of the two Earth men.

It was at once evident that the gigantic city was built in a huge bubble, perhaps twenty miles in diameter. The stem-like buildings that stretched upward to impossible heights also stretched downward to the bottom of the bubble, miles below; and the roadway on which they stood struck out toward the nearest building, almost half a mile away.

Gar grinned at Turlogh. "You might as well stop packing that toy around," he said, pointing at the submachine gun. "It won't do anything but get us into trouble. We're either living on borrowed time already or there is probably a welcoming committee, just around the corner someplace, waiting for us to lay down this gun and show signs of being good."

"You may be right," Turlogh admitted. "We stand about as much chance of doing some good with this gun as a gangster would have against the whole United States Government. The sensible thing for us to do is turn right around and get out of here until we can bring enough people with us to stand a chance. I think we could make it if we jammed that airlock by wedging the outer door open as we left."

"I'll bet you a hundred to one our ship is swarming with these foreigners right now," Gar said.

"Maybe so," Turlogh answered. "They probably have several airlocks to the surface."

THEY climbed back into the car and moved slowly out into the bubble, watching the road ahead for signs of the welcoming committee they were sure was ahead.

"Do you think it possible for a bubble like this to form in solid rock," Gar asked thoughtfully, "with the gas that caused the bubble being made up of breathable air, evolve life that eventually produces a civilization like this one, keeping normal temperatures over millions of years? Or do you think this race moved into the bubble and made it over, including the atmosphere, and imported atomic power from someplace?"

"It's certain they moved in," Turlogh replied. "The metals for their machinery, the water necessary to produce life, and the power necessary to keep this thing running, all have to be imported. The question in *my* mind is whether this race originated on Pluto, or came from some other planet. I'm wondering if it is possible that deep down in Pluto there might be huge caverns where life originated and evolved into an intelligent race.

"Take those airlocks, for example. Could a race evolved here conceive of the vacuum of outer space? Or would they open a shaft to the surface and let their air escape? I think this race must have come from some other planet and picked this bubble for a colony. No doubt the other warm spots are also over similar colonies."

"No doubt about that now?" Gar commented. Then spying a figure standing in the middle of the road far ahead, "Look! At last we contact the enemy. Don't shoot till you see the mottled red of their eyes."

He speeded up the car slightly, and both men kept their eyes fixed on the figure ahead, intensely curious as to what the appearance of these unknown creatures would be like.

The figure as they drew closer turned out to be that of an ordinary man, arm raised in a signal for them to stop. Gar brought the car to a stop about ten feet in front of the man. He was dressed in the same kind of clothes as were Gar and Turlogh. His face was conventional, with a welcoming smile on it.

Behind him the road branched off to disappear through the wall of one of the buildings. After the car came to a stop the man lowered his arm and walked forward to meet them. His voice, normal and friendly, called out, "Hello, there. Welcome to Bubble City."

"Hello yourself," Gar answered, "I didn't know that the United States had a colony on Pluto. When did all this take place?"

The man reached the side of the car and extended his hand, saying, "My name is Gar Hogan."

"Gar Hogan!" exclaimed Gar. "My name is Gar Nickols and my partner's is Turlogh Hogan. Don't tell me your first name is mine and your last name is Turlogh's!"

"By a strange coincidence," the stranger said, smiling, "it is." Then, stepping on the running board of the car and pointing toward the opening in the building, he added, "Won't you step into my parlor?"

Gar gave him a quizzical look and started the car. Then casually he asked, "Don't you have a sister back in New Jersey named Doris?"

"Sister?" the stranger asked, puzzled. "What's a sister?"

Gar stopped the car. "Look," he said resignedly. "I don't know who or what you are, but I know you are not a human being."

The stranger who called himself Gar Hogan stepped down from the running board, the welcoming smile still painted on his face, as though he knew no other expression.

"But I *am* human," he said earnestly. "Perhaps not human like you two are; but human just the same."

"What do you mean by that?" Turlogh asked. He now had the gun pointed at the chest of the stranger, ready to pull the trigger.

THE STRANGER shrugged his shoulders. "You have machines and various robot forms to do work for you. So do we. In your minds I have seen huge ships that sail on vast pools of liquid, long strings of track-riding carriers, and all the other signs of intelligence. It is a different kind of world than this in our bubble, and so great that you cannot fill it completely."

"Go on," Gar said. His mind was in a strange turmoil of suspicions which he could not pin down, fears as from some danger only instinctively felt, and puzzlement.

The stranger smiled vaguely now, but continued. "With all these similarities we are still far apart. In your mind is a queer set of vague, amoeba-like fears and instincts. Illogical thought processes fill your thinking. The urge to destroy as a means of perpetuating the robot figures you are now inhabiting leads me to suspect they are the only ones you have. Yet that would be the height of foolishness, to go on an interplanetary voyage such as you have, without spares and specialized bodies for different tasks."

The stranger frowned for the first time. His frown was clumsy and appeared slowly in a disconnected pattern, one face muscle after another moving exploratively until it settled into the pattern of a frown. Gar and Turlogh watched this transition of expression with horrified fascination. It seemed almost as if the stranger's face were being molded into a new shape by some unseen sculptor. Then he spoke again.

"Every sign points to something so strange and startling that I can't trust my conclusion. All the evidence points to your minds being entirely contained within the compass of your present bodies. I read in your minds the conviction that if your present bodies are destroyed you yourselves are destroyed! Am I right?"

"Not exactly," Turlogh answered him.

The stranger looked at him intently for a moment. "Oh, I see," he said. "You believe that the thinking entity that is you will be preserved after the destruction of this machine it lives in, but without recourse to other such machines. No? Oh. You have different theories about it. Hmm. Very interesting. But at the foundation of each theory is the assumption—the conviction, I should say—that this psyche, or soul, resides *in* the body it directs, I wonder if that can be true in your case?"

"What makes that sound so unbelievable?" asked Gar.

"Perhaps just the newness of it," the stranger replied. "With me it is different. And I wonder if you might not be mistaken about your nature? I inhabit thousands of bodies at the same time. Or rather, I don't inhabit them, but am aware *through* them. To be sure, they are strictly mechanical, while yours seems to be organic in structure. That is new to me also. Each of my units of awareness and action has its own sets of reflexes, and its own focus of awareness. Yet I am able to concentrate my over-all awareness in just one of them as I am doing now, as well as spread it out over all of them and carry on thousands of independent trains of thought simultaneously. I was just wondering, suppose I myself were without awareness, but my thought processes continued just as always, but would be ignorant of my true functioning in relation to them. Hmm..."

"Then," Turlogh exclaimed. "You are in effect a mass consciousness!"

"No," he answered. "Not a mass consciousness. My vehicle of existence is not the bodies I direct, but independent of them. If every body I have in action, and all those in reserve, were to be destroyed, I would continue to exist. And I am wondering if perhaps you are not, or could not be made to be the same!"

"You mean you are a spirit, or a disembodied intelligence?" asked Gar.

"No. I see what you mean. But my vehicle of existence is quite material." He became silent.

CHAPTER THREE

STRANGE thoughts began to run through Turlogh's mind. Each of the tall, reed-like buildings housed a gigantic brain. Each was an individual entity, and the millions of moving figures that swarmed the ribbon-like roads that swung from building to building were just the arms, eyes, feelers, and instruments of the vast, unmoving brains in these buildings!

The same thoughts were coursing through Gar's mind.

The two men looked at the buildings with new interest.

"How did all this begin?" asked Gar.

The stranger put his foot on the running board of the car in a purely human gesture. "We don't know," he answered simply. "Logic tells us that if we had no moving units we could not make them. Logic tells us that at one time we must have been different. But, as a matter of fact, none of us can remember when we first began. Our minds, as they grew in awareness, found the robot units already in existence, and machines for their manufacture already operating. We could like it to be. For example, change the type of robot that was made merely by imagining what we would like it to be. For example, the figure standing before you is an imitation of your own figures."

"Has it ever occurred to you that you might have yourself been built by humans such as we are?" asked Turlogh.

"No," he answered slowly. "As a matter of fact you are a new concept to us. It has never occurred to us that there might be living creatures able to reproduce that were each moving beings with self-contained thinking powers."

"How long do you know you have existed?" asked Gar.

"We don't know that, either," he replied. "We had awareness for perhaps a million of your Earth years before we finally knew our own nature. As a matter of fact, we passed through much the same stages in our thinking as you seem to be going through. At one time we each thought the seat of intelligence was in the body and kept on after the destruction of the body. It took us a million years to realize we were the buildings and what they contain. Even then your planet was still glowing with its own self light."

"That's interesting," Turlogh said. "You say that you at one time had the same theories about reincarnation, immortality, and so forth that we now have?"

"Not exactly," the stranger replied. "You see, we always had complete memory of our former lives. Also, our consciousness extended to many robots at the same time. We did have a theory that we were the mass awareness of several individuals, a sort of spiritual fluid that flowed from one mind to another. In fact, we had mental battles for possession of all the robots for thousands of years of your time until we turned our thoughts inward and studied the details of our structure and discovered that such struggles were meaningless, since we could get any number of robot bodies we wished by a simple act of will, from our own selves.

"You have no memory extending beyond your present body, nor does your awareness extend to other bodies. Yet that may be due to your incomplete development.

"We of the bubble would like to conduct tests to determine your nature. We would like to do that because it might reveal our own origin."

"What kind of tests?" asked Turlogh suspiciously.

"Tests in shielding," the stranger replied. "If your entity is completely self-contained they will have no effect. If they are still back on Earth, then complete shielding will cut off their contact with the body so that it ceases to think."

GAR AND Turlogh looked at each other. There was uncertainty and lingering suspicion of this stranger in their glance, and a dawning interest in the whole bizarre mystery of this strange bubble civilization.

"What do you think?" Gar asked Turlogh.

"I'm wondering if we shouldn't conduct a few tests of our own first," Turlogh replied.

"For example?" Gar queried.

"Blasting this fellow out of existence as I did in my dream," Turlogh grinned. "If that doesn't make him mad, then he is all he claims."

"How would it be if we just made a break for it and got away from this place?" Gar suggested a trifle wistfully.

"I doubt if we could," Turlogh answered. "This car is probably one of their robot bodies. I can see now that they made it in imitation of our memories of surface cars on Earth. They sucked us in neatly just like in the old tale of the wolf that put on a sheep skin to wander into the flock and pick out a victim."

"This place gives me the creeps," Gar said. "Maybe even the road is intelligent, and would curl up in front of us if we tried to get away. Suppose we make a deal with them."

"What kind of a deal?" asked Turlogh.

"One of us go back to the ship and the other stay for the tests. Then if something happens whichever one of us is in the ship can blast a hole in this bubble and at least get revenge."

Turlogh thought this over for a moment. "O.K.," he said.

"That is O.K. with me, too," the stranger put in. "I'm convinced you are rational enough to not be a threat to our existence so long as we do not destroy either of you."

Turlogh pulled a coin out of his pocket and said hastily. "I'll take heads."

Gar quickly grabbed the coin and looked at it. Just as he suspected, it was the double-headed nickel that Turlogh carried around for a good luck piece.

"O.K., O.K., Turlogh chuckled. "We'll make it honest."

Gar gave him back the nickel and reached in his own pocket, looking questioningly at his partner.

"I'll still take heads," Turlogh said.

With a quiet grin which he tried to hide, Gar flipped a coin in the air. It landed on the roadway outside the car. The two men leaned over to look at it.

"Tails!" Gar exclaimed triumphantly, and climbed out to retrieve his coin. Straightening up, he slipped the coin back into his pocket and said softly, "So long, Turlogh."

The car, now of its own volition, turned and sped back into the tunnel. Gar watched it go, the hand in his pocket idly fingering two coins; one, a quarter with two heads, the other a half dollar with two tails. When the car vanished from sight he turned and walked toward the entrance to the tall building, the stranger following.

Inside, about twenty feet from the outside wall, were several pillars six or seven feet in diameter, placed in an orderly row. One of these had a section of its side swung back, exposing a smooth bore, and a flat surfaced disc of a floor, even with the floor outside.

The stranger stepped inside, followed by Gar. Noiselessly the opening closed. At the same time Gar suddenly felt weightless. This weightlessness lasted for almost a full minute. Then it was replaced by tremendous weight that seemed to bear every atom of his body toward the floor.

As he fought the pressure his mind put the evidence of his senses together. This must be an elevator. It had at first been sinking in almost free fall. Now it was coming to a gradual stop at an acceleration of about three gees. To verify his conclusion the walls of the cylinder, which had been perfectly smooth with the blurred smoothness of terrific speed, began to show irregularities that rose from the floor and disappeared far up the shaft.

The piston came to a stop and the wall swung out again to reveal a scene which was the exact duplicate of the one above that they had left. Already Gar knew he was lost. The floors were not numbered in any way and there were thousands of them.

Now Gar followed the stranger along the inside wall of the building, passed through a swinging door with him, and entered a vast laboratory. Strange transparent monstrosities were all about him. Huge vats with bubbling liquids, almost familiar looking tangles of wires and vacuum tubes, and long rows of instrument panels.

Several queer looking robots were wheeling a large square box into the room from the other end. The man motioned Gar to enter through the small door in its front. Gar did so, with him following. Inside was a desk and a chair. On the desk was a writing pad and a pencil.

"You will start writing," the stranger said. "It doesn't matter what you write just so long as you keep on writing steadily. We will soon be completely insulated from the outside. I will cease to be conscious of what goes on in here. If you are self-contained you will not lose consciousness. The evidence of what you have written will be proof."

Gar sat down and started to write.

TURLOGH reached the airlock without mishap. It was just as they had left it. He hooked up the valve lever again and entered the lock, donning his vacuum suit before closing the inner door.

As the outer door swung open he stepped out, and with a single backward glance climbed up the slope to the space ship. It, too, had been untouched since they left it.

Inside once again he took off his vacuum suit and hastily made the rounds on an inspection tour. Everything was just as they had left it.

Now doubts began to assail him. This bubble city seemed too pat and too advanced. Building a creature, a robot that looked human and talked the language they themselves used, took the workings of a very superior mentality. One so superior that they could not hope to outguess it.

On the spur of the moment he decided to blast off from the surface and resume the old orbit around the planet. Then it would be possible to escape and notify the Earth of this strange race if something sinister developed. At most it would mean a delay of only a few hours in picking up Gar, and Gar would approve of his precautions.

Long ago he and Gar had considered the possibility of a situation similar to the present one, and decided that the safety of future explorers was of more importance than the life of one of them. And Gar could contact the ship by radio once he put his vacuum suit on again.

The next eight hours was spent in the takeoff and the almost dainty spurts from the rockets that put him back in the original orbit. By the time the tablerock in the center of the warm spot again came into sight, the ship was an inert, swiftly moving satellite of Pluto once more.

Turlogh had put the ship into orbits around nearly every planet in the system, and each time he had the same thought. If he were to die the ship would circle endlessly forever unless somebody collided with it.

As the tablerock flashed by below he examined it through the ship telescope. Gar had not come up yet. It would be another eight hours, thirty seven minutes, and ten seconds, before the spot would be visible from the ship again.

Turlogh yawned. Turning the radio receiver on to the suit wavelength, so that it would wake him up if Gar should try to contact him, he undressed and stretched out in his bunk. Soon he slept. This time his sleep was dreamless.

GAR KEPT on writing even after the stranger slumped to the floor unconscious. He wrote whatever came into his head, Lincoln's Gettysburg Address, nursery rhymes, and whatever came to mind. After half an hour the stranger stirred, then rose to his feet.

He read closely what Gar had written. Then he opened the small door and stepped outside, motioning Gar to follow him.

"One more test," he said in a matter of fact tone, "and then we will be satisfied."

Another machine had been wheeled into the room. It was a chair with a hood for the head, something like those in beauty parlors back on Earth.

Confidently Gar sat down and allowed the stranger to lower the hood over his head. Almost the next instant, it seemed, the hood was lifted.

He stood up and swayed dizzily. The stranger caught him, and supported him until the wave of dizziness passed. After that one spell his mind cleared like magic. His senses seemed much sharper than they ever had been before.

"We are completely satisfied," the stranger said smiling. "You may now return to your friend in his ship. I believe he is circling the planet in your original exploration orbit. It is now just fifty minutes before he will reach the plateau again so that you can contact him."

"Thanks," Gar said vaguely, "I'd better get up there right away then where I can talk to him and let him know I'm O.K."

The stranger led him to the elevator, back up to the roadway, and waved a friendly farewell as a car bore Gar toward the surface lock. There Gar found his vacuum suit and was soon climbing the slope back to the tablerock.

He turned on the suit radio and tried to contact Turlogh. When he was halfway up the slope the ship appeared over the horizon as a slowly moving star. Almost immediately Turlogh's voice sounded.

"Hello. Am I glad to see you down there! Better take a nap in the airlock to the bubble, because I have to go around again to land," Turlogh said.

Gar stopped his climb. "Guess you're right," he answered. "It'll be almost nine hours before you land. I don't feel sleepy, but I can't stand out here that long."

"How did everything go?" asked Turlogh anxiously.

"O.K., I guess." Gar said. "I'm a little lost mentally. They seem only interested in determining that I am completely self-contained. They seem satisfied on that now, so they have lost interest in us."

"That's funny," Turlogh said slowly. "It would seem that they would be anxious to get better acquainted with us. But I'd just as soon scram out of here if it is O.K. with you, Gar. We can't get any radioactives here, and that's what we came for. Maybe we'd just better hand in a report on Earth and forget the whole thing. Huh?"

"Maybe so," Gar replied, turning and starting back toward the airlock.

Once there, he opened the front plate on his suit and relaxed. Almost instantly he was asleep.

And almost instantly he began to dream...

He felt queer and helpless. He was sprawled out on a smooth floor. The images of his surroundings seemed queerly distorted. Gradually they came into focus and became sensible.

He tried to get up. A queer, thrashing feeling shook his body. He turned his head to see what caused it and saw that his body was a long thing with several legs. Horror made him wake up. He did not move, but quietly felt of the comforting closeness of his vacuum suit, and let his eyes wander around the airlock to reassure his mind of his surroundings.

CHAPTER FOUR

WHEN HE went back to sleep and the dream continued, it seemed all right for his dream body to have many legs. As if playing a game he moved them experimentally and found that if he concentrated on just the front legs the others always followed suit in a definite rhythm.

Having so many legs made him remember the old joke about the thousand legged worm and the beetle. The beetle asks the worm how he can keep so many legs moving without getting mixed up, and the worm says, "It's easy, I'll show you." So he concentrates on his legs and gets all mixed up. Forever after he stumbles, Gar chuckled in his dream, and walked around the room quite expertly by forgetting all about the back legs and concentrating only on the front ones.

In front of him was a mirror. He stopped in front of it and looked at his dream body. Its reflection in the mirror seemed real. He thought, "As long as I'm having such a screwy dream I might as well try something. I'll transfer my consciousness to the image in the mirror and see how I actually look," Instantly he was looking at another figure; that of a spiderlike creature.

But he could still see the many legged one too. He seemed to be seeing with the eyes of both creatures at once, and the sensation of looking at himself from two bodies, and being in those two bodies, gave his mind a jerk, as though his personality were splitting and his brain with it. He woke up and climbed to his feet.

"If I go back to sleep I'll go nuts," he muttered drowsily, clamping the face plate of his suit back in place. His wrist watch showed he had been asleep four hours. Stepping out of the air lock he began a leisurely climb up the long slope toward the tablerock, resolved not to sleep again until this crazy planet was just a dot in the sky, and good old Earth was on the nose of the ship.

A seemingly black cloud shooting up from the horizon to occult a large area of the star blanketed sky, signaled the arrival of the space ship before it appeared. Gar stayed in the protection of the large boulder near the top of the slope until the ship landed, then finished his climb to the ship.

Inside he hastily took off his vacuum suit and strapped himself in a recoil chair beside his partner, who then blasted off. The ship had rested on the planet just eleven minutes.

With the gyro stabilizers keeping the nose of the ship pointed away from the planet, and the stern rockets spurting a constant blast of four gees, the ship spiraled outward until Pluto became a vanishing dot in the heavens.

While this was going on Gar told the details of his strange dream to Turlogh, whose only comment was, "If we ever come here again we will both go nuts. To hell with space travel. When we get home I'm going to find a nice quiet spot and spend the rest of my life fishing."

He said it as if he meant it.

While Turlogh was correcting the ship's course so that its free flight orbit would intersect the Earth's orbit at the right spot, Gar typed out a complete report on their visit to Pluto. Then both men turned in.

Turlogh lay in his bunk thinking of Gar's dream for a long time after he heard Gar's quiet snoring. A worried frown creased his forehead.

Gar went to sleep the moment he stretched out in his bunk. And again he dreamt. In the dream he seemed to reverse things. His recent wakefulness, the takeoff from Pluto, Turlogh—all seemed like something he had dreamed while asleep, and his awareness through the two strange bodies in the large room seemed the reality.

HIS CONSCIOUSNESS seemed to split quite naturally into two separate and independent parts, one in the many legged worm, and the other in the spiderlike body. Almost like two separate individuals he sent each body on an exploring trip around the room, the worm found a door and pushed it open to reveal another large room in which several other bodies were parked, each different in shape, and obviously designed for different duties. A third focus of consciousness seemed to split off in his mind, and suddenly he could see this room from the position a humanoid body with flexible arms and many fingered hands occupied. He turned the head downward, and sure enough he was seeing that body as if it were his own, while at the same time he could see it from the eyes of the many legged worm.

"This is interesting work," he thought to himself.

He began to play a game. First he would concentrate all his consciousness in one of the bodies. Then he would concentrate it in another, exploring the capabilities of each.

Finally he tried to see how many of these bodies he could control and be aware through at once. There seemed no limit. A simple act of will created a whole new focus of consciousness, complete with visual, auditory, and reasoning centers.

From a great distance he heard a soft jangling that had a vague familiarity about it. One part of his mind puzzled over it while he was gazing with rapt attention at one of his bodies through the eyes of several of the others, and coordinating all the images into completely three dimensional images in his consciousness. It was fascinating to have a solid object seem to actually exist in its entirety in his mind.

That part of his mind that was puzzling over the bell suddenly remembered that it was the alarm in his bunk. He opened his eyes to the familiar surroundings of the ship. *The dream did not stop.*

His mind had split again, and the part that was Gar was on the ship, while the dozens of other foci of consciousness in the various dream bodies continued without interruption!

He lay in the bunk thinking with one part of his mind. It was all clear now. He was no longer just Gar Nichols. Under that machine on Pluto he had become one of the Bubble men. How, he didn't know.

The part of him that was Gar stretched lazily and climbed out of the bunk. Turlogh was already up, so he dressed slowly, trying to decide whether he should tell his partner or not.

He decided not to until he found out more. First he must find out whether his brain had been taken out of his skull and set in some vat in one of the buildings in Bubble City, or if there had merely been some change made in his brain so that it could direct and be aware through robot bodies on Pluto while still occupying his own body.

That would make all the difference in the world, for if the latter were the case he could forget about the bodies on Pluto and remain just Gar Nichols; but if the former were the case he was sunk. Or was he? Could he go on being Gar in one small part of his mind until his Earth body died of old age, while at the same time he lived a fuller, many faceted life as a Plutonian? If that were what was in store for him it wouldn't be half bad.

A new angle occurred to him. If his brain were on Pluto his reflexes should slow down, because it would take time for impulses to travel from Pluto to the ship as it got farther and farther away.

"How far are we from Pluto now?" he asked Turlogh casually between bites of ham and eggs at breakfast.

Instantly Turlogh replied, "About a million and a half."

There was no time lag perceptible above the norm, Gar performed a little mental arithmetic. About nine seconds for light to reach them from Pluto. That should mean a time lag of eighteen seconds. It wasn't there, so—

Other parts of his multiple consciousness took up the problem. There was no time lag for his bodies on Pluto either! The part of his mind that was aware through the spider robot set out to find a robot of one of the other Bubble creatures.

HE FOUND a door that opened out onto one of the suspended roadways and made his way to the nearest building. Halfway there a robot left that building and came to meet him.

Speaking in English it said, "I see that you have finally found out about yourself. Are you mad at us?"

"I don't know," Gar replied. "Where's my brain? In my body on the space ship, or in the building I just left?"

"In the building," was the answer. "That is, part of it is. The bulk of the Gar personality and the seat of consciousness were removed, leaving only the sections necessary to the functioning of your old body. When it dies you will still retain all your memories of your life as Gar Nichols, and while it lives you will be able to continue as Gar Nichols without any trouble."

"But how about time lag?" asked Gar.

"Time lag?" the robot asked. "Oh, I see what you mean. There is no appreciable time lag. Telepathy takes place by means of waves in the ether, which travel at the speed of about two hundred billion miles a second."

"Huh?" Gar exclaimed.

"It's like this," the robot explained. "Suppose you have an electron and a proton stuck together. In a line directed outward from the pair, in a direction such that the proton completely hides the electron, the field is positive. In the opposite direction it is completely negative. Give the pair a spinning motion, and every time it goes completely around, the electrical field in one direction has gone through one change from positive to negative to positive. If there is an electron somewhere it will be attracted, repelled, and again attracted, so that its movement will be slightly oscillating."

"Hmm," Said Gar thoughtfully, his eyes idly watching a column of moving figures on a road below.

"These alternating waves of attraction and repulsion," the robot figure before him went on, "travel through the ether at the square root of the mean square velocity of the ether particles, which is about two hundred billion miles a second. Light travels at a hundred and eighty-six thousand miles a second because it is electron-proton in structure, and travels because of the unbalanced ether pressures against the electrons and the protons. An entirely different thing."

"Then I'll have no difficulty being myself when the ship lands on Earth?" asked Gar.

"We can't guarantee anything," the robot replied, "but we think you will have no trouble at all."

"How is it possible for one mind to be aware through several bodies without getting everything mixed up?" asked Gar.

"In *one* body you have visual centers, auditory centers, etc.," the robot explained. "All of these operate without interfering with one another. You can be aware of what you see, hear, feel, taste, and smell, all at the same time. Creatures such as the reptiles and fowls on Earth, which have independently functioning eyes, have two independent visual centers. It's just an extension of the same thing to have many bodies."

The robot hesitated for a minute, then said, "We have found out many things about ourselves by this experiment on you. Undoubtedly we were once living creatures just as you were. The parts of our makeup that were mysteries to us before are no longer that."

DURING the long journey back to Earth Gar had plenty of time to relax, as Gar, and concentrate most of his mental energies on expanding his abilities in Bubble City.

Turlogh suspected nothing, and as the days wore on and Gar seemed to have no more dreams, or at least did not mention having any more, the strangeness of their experiences on Pluto dimmed. It took him by surprise when Gar awoke from a daydream two days out from Earth and casually remarked that he had decided to retire from space travel and get a place in the country where he could work on a few gadgets he had been thinking about.

All the suspicions he had had for the first few days on their journey outward from Pluto returned, but he shrugged his shoulders and remarked that it was a good idea. "I think I'll retire myself," he added. Then, grinning, "I think with Pluto we've seen about everything."

"Ah—Turlogh," Gar said after several minutes of silence.

"Yeah?" Turlogh prompted.

"Ah—about the report on Bubble City," Gar hesitated. "Suppose we don't hand that in, I just want to retire and live in peace, and if we turned that loose we would be on the front pages of every paper in the world and pestered to death to lead an expedition back there."

"Sure, sure," Turlogh said soothingly. "I agree with you. We're rich now and can do what we want. Fame would spoil it."

Out of the corner of his eye he saw Gar sigh with relief. He got up and went forward to peer through the forward telescope at the swiftly growing Earth. A gong sounded, and he hastened to the shock seats with Gar. Almost as soon as they had strapped themselves in, the first deceleration blast shook the ship.

Twenty hours later the ship settled in its berth at the Arizona space port. As the two men stepped to the ground a decrepit taxi wheezed up.

Gar climbed in, but Turlogh shook his head. "You go on into Denver, Gar, I'll fill out the trip sheet in the office." He winked at Gar to let him know he had not forgotten about keeping silent about Bubble City. Gar winked back and nodded his agreement.

Turlogh's stride was determined and resolute as he made his way across the field to the office buildings. The job ahead would be a disagreeable one to him.

He made a long distance phone call and then relaxed over a huge steak in the cafe. An hour and a half later a slim jet plane dipped out of the sky and came to a stop outside. Turlogh went out to meet its passenger, a skinny man six feet tall with a grey tweed suit. They shook hands.

"I'm Mr. Foster," the skinny man introduced himself. "The office assigned me to the case. They said you have a story to tell that is so fantastic it won't be believed."

"That's right," Turlogh said. "And I may not have another chance to repeat it, so I'd better tell it where it will go on a spool for future reference."

CHAPTER FIVE

AN HOUR later he was bringing his account to an end. Leaning back in a swivel chair, his feet on a desk, he held a microphone to his lips while Mr. Foster sat across the desk and made occasional notes in a little book.

"There are several things that make me think Gar has become a robot of those creatures on Pluto," Turlogh was summing up his story. "First, Gar never used to go right to sleep. Now he is asleep the second his head hits the pillow. Second, he has always kept busy on other trips, making various gadgets, reading, and hounding me to death to play chess with him. On our trip from Pluto he did none of these things. He kept to himself, spent most of his time napping or just staring at nothing, and seldom spoke except to answer me.

"And now he plans to retire and make a few gadgets he has in mind. What are they? We have never had any secrets before! He wants to keep it secret that there are intelligent beings of some kind on Pluto. Why? Why all these changes in character of a man I have known for years? Why his secrecy? Why the polite hints that after this trip I was to go my own way and let him go his alone?

"I think he should be watched carefully all the time," he went on. "My theory is that he is now a robot instrument of the Plutonians. They plan to conquer the Earth. If that's correct, then Gar will set up a laboratory to make more robots, or make robots out of men. And he will build machines to rule the world with."

He laid down the microphone and sat up. Mr. Foster looked back over his notes for a few minutes in silence.

"He didn't make anything on the ship or bring anything with him from Pluto did he?" he finally asked.

"No," Turlogh replied. "Unless it was so small he could conceal it in his clothing. Anyway, he was still the old Gar when I picked him up and blasted off, except for the strange dream he had had in the airlock on Pluto."

"Well," Mr. Foster said, rising to his feet. "We will keep a constant watch on him and examine everything he buys in the way of materials. He won't be able to build anything that will be a threat to us. Meanwhile, keep in touch with me. Just call the number on that card I gave you and ask for me."

"O.K.," Turlogh answered. The two men shook hands gravely and parted.

GAR WAS worried, and whenever he was worried he found something to keep him busy. Two days out from Earth he had relaxed in his bunk, closed his eyes, and left his body to itself, while he concentrated all his mental faculties on mastery of his dozens of robots in Bubble City, confident that when the alarm clock went off he would be able to regain awareness through his old body as usual.

Yet after several hours when he tried to contact his old body he couldn't get the slightest response. Immediately he had sent one of his robots out to get the robot of the stranger, the "Gar Hogan" who seemed to have no name of his own.

They met on the roadway again, and Gar burst out with the information that he had lost contact with his body on the ship.

"That's too bad," the stranger sympathized. "But there is nothing we can do about it now. If Turlogh senses the nature of the trouble he may turn back. If he doesn't, your body will go on living, but without any guiding intelligence it may run into trouble."

"What'll I do?" asked Gar frantically.

"Just forget about it," the stranger advised. "You are here. You have millions of years ahead of you. You will soon forget about your Earth body."

"I don't want to forget about it," Gar cried. "Don't you realize that without my Earth body I don't give a damn about all this?"

"But there is nothing you can do about it," the stranger spoke sadly.

"I'll go mad," Gar said wildly. "I don't want to spend a million years playing with grotesque bodies like a child with paper dolls."

"I'll make you a promise," the stranger said sympathetically. "We will try to re-establish contact with your body. If we can't, in not over a year you will see Earth again in a body that looks and acts exactly like your original one. We will help you build a ship, under your direction, to take it to Earth. Will that satisfy you?"

"I guess it'll have to," Gar answered despondently.

The stranger looked at him speculatively for a moment and then turned around and went back to his own building.

Gar watched him go, and then did the same, feeling like a turtle drawing its head into its shell.

Back in his building again he built a worm body a city block long with two thousand legs. All he had to do was think of the details and his robot machinery turned it out. When it was finished he started out on a journey of exploration of the bubble, gliding along on the roadways, swinging over the edge and dropping to lower roadways.

After one got used to it the city was monotonous in its regularity. The buildings were evenly spaced, and all of the same architecture. They were all tied together by the networks of suspended roadways at every fifty foot level, from the bottom of the bubble to the top; and the foundations of each building were as solidly imbedded in the native rock at the top as at the bottom, so that the entire bubble was more or less an architectural and structural unit.

GAR, IN his bizarre robot body, was left strictly alone. Although he passed hundreds of robots they passed him without pausing. Even when he finally spoke to one he was ignored. In a fit of anger he pushed the robot he had spoken to over the edge of the roadway and watched it turn slowly over and over as it dropped to the bottom of the bubble.

He fully expected this act to bring out some sort of response from the impassive minds of the city; but so far as he could see, no one paid the slightest attention to his warlike act.

He followed a group of robots in an attempt to learn what there was to do around the city. They wandered ant like from level to level, apparently having no definite purpose in their wanderings.

At last he gave up in disgust and returned to his own building. "It's like being the last guest at a summer resort after the first snowfall," he muttered to himself.

Turlogh caught a taxi into Denver after watching the secret service man's jet plane disappear toward the east. He and Gar were part owners of the Stratford Hotel, and kept one suite of rooms for themselves.

Turlogh stopped at the desk and asked if Gar had come in yet. The clerk said he had gone up half an hour before, so Turlogh stepped into the waiting elevator and rode to the fifth floor.

The door to the apartment was unlocked. Turlogh pushed it open and walked in, Gar was sitting at the desk phoning.

His side of the conversation was noncommittal, consisting mostly of "I see's" and "O.K.'s." With a last "O.K," he hung up.

"Get through all the red tape?" he asked.

"Yeah," Turlogh grunted.

There was a discreet knock at the door, and Gar rose to let in the boy with a tray and several newspapers.

"Want some?" asked Gar.

"I'll have a pot of coffee," Turlogh said, picking up one of the newspapers. He retired to a window corner and left Gar to himself. Gar began his meal with perfect composure, as if Turlogh ignoring him were the most natural thing in the world.

He finished his meal just as the boy returned with Turlogh's coffee. With a muttered, "Guess I'll go out for a while," he followed the boy out into the hall, closing the door without a backward glance.

Turlogh stepped hastily to the phone and dialed a number the secret service man had given him. Almost at once the other end answered. Turlogh told them that Gar had just left the room and was probably in the lobby by now. Then he hung up.

It was shortly after that that Gar disappeared. Turlogh was told all about it that evening. Gar had been followed from the hotel. He went directly to a luggage store where he bought a small suitcase. From there he went directly to the First National Bank to the safety deposit vault. When Turlogh heard of this he felt sick. He and Gar kept a cash fund of over twenty million dollars in their safety deposit box.

From the bank he had gone to the surgical supply house in the medical and dental building, leaving there with a package which inquiry later on disclosed to have contained most of the instruments necessary for a brain surgery.

WHEN he left the surgical supply company he hopped into a cruising cab, and was out of sight before the secret service man following him could get one. He noted the number of the cab, though, and found out later that it had taken Gar to a downtown corner. He had paid his fare and vanished in the crowd of afternoon shoppers. There the trail vanished.

An emergency dragnet was put around the city, but Gar had had over two hours to pick up a car and leave before every car was being stopped. The Denver police were called in to help. Every car dealer in the city was shown Gar's picture before the day was over, but none of them had seen him.

The picture was run on the front page of the morning paper with a five hundred dollar reward for information of any kind.

Turlogh went with the secret service man to the bank the next morning and opened the deposit box. It was empty.

"Do you have any record of the numbers of the bills?" asked Fred Ginther, the secret service man.

"No," Turlogh replied. "We kept that money as a sort of emergency fund."

"I see," Fred Ginther said dryly. "That accounts for almost two percent of all the money that has been kept out of circulation for the past ten years!"

"You never know when you'll need large sums of money in a hurry. That's why we kept it," Turlogh replied uncomfortably.

Two weeks went by. Then one day Gar was picked up in the loop in Chicago. He was picked up because he didn't know who he was or where he was, and because he was standing in the middle of the street looking around blankly at the stalled cars.

The traffic cop led him to the curb and called the wagon. At police headquarters he was unable to answer any question rationally.

Only then did the police look into it more closely and find that they had picked up Gar Nichols. They sent a wire to the Denver police who had put out the reward notice.

Turlogh and Fred Ginther caught the next plane to Chicago. When they entered the room where Gar was being detained he was sitting on a bench, staring blankly across the room at the opposite wall. He turned his head at their entrance, but showed no sign of recognition when he looked at Turlogh.

"This him?" Fred asked tersely.

Turlogh nodded wordlessly. Then he turned and left the room. Fred asked Gar a few questions. Getting no response he followed Turlogh who was at the desk asking questions.

Gar had had no suitcase on him when picked up. There were no papers in his pocket of any kind. He had on the clothes he left Denver in. That was all.

"What do you think has happened," Fred asked Turlogh.

"I hate to say what I think has happened," Turlogh replied. "I think you'd better get your boss here."

Fred lifted the nearest phone from its cradle and asked for long distance.

Turlogh was pacing angrily up and down in his hotel room on the twenty-third floor of the Palmer house. Fred Ginther and the skinny man were slouched calmly in the two armchairs the hotel provided each tenant.

"Take it easy, Turlogh," Fred said soothingly.

"Take it easy!" Turlogh exclaimed. "We've got to go back to Pluto and drop a couple of bombs on that bubble before something happens so we can't."

"What can happen?" the skinny man asked.

"What can happen?" Turlogh echoed. "Why, lots can happen. Don't you see what's happened already?"

"Sure. Your partner has lost his memory. You say that these things in the bubble on Pluto operated on him and took over." The skinny man paused speculatively. "Let's assume that's the case. Then one of the things was here on Earth. He evidently lost control or else gave it up as a bad job after finding our civilization much bigger than he had thought. What could he do as one man that would threaten the whole world?"

"It's perfectly obvious what he did. He got those surgical instruments didn't he?" Turlogh exclaimed.

"So what?" Fred Ginther said.

"That thing that was controlling Gar's body operated on somebody else to make a robot out of him." Turlogh emphasized each word. "Right now somebody we don't know and have no way of finding out is a robot body of these things on Pluto. If it were friendly it wouldn't resort to such means and take such pains to cover up. And don't forget, *those things are millions of years old.* Our science is puny compared to what they probably know. If we don't destroy them right away it may be too late."

THE PHONE rang. The skinny man picked it up and said, "Foster speaking." He listened for a minute and then hung up. His eyes held a thoughtful look as he absently dropped the phone in its cradle.

"You may be right at that," he finally murmured. "An x-ray shows a small metal object of complex outline at the base of Gar's skull, imbedded in the brain."

"Is the brain all there?" asked Turlogh hastily.

"No," Mr. Foster said slowly. "The frontal lobe is missing. The space it should occupy is filled with a paraffin substance. Also a few cubic centimeters of the back part of the brain is out, where that metal object is located."

He stared moodily at the carpet for several minutes. Then he gave a disgruntled snort. "At any rate," he said, "we can no longer doubt your story, no matter how unbelievable it sounds."

"What are we going to do?" asked Turlogh.

"It looks like we'll have to make a few atom bombs, but that'll take time. At least a month. Meanwhile we'll alert the whole police system, both local and government."

He pulled out a cigar and bit the end off savagely. "We have the best electronic experts in the world on the way to Chicago now. They're going to examine that gadget in your partner's skull to see if they can find out what it is. And the best surgeons in the country are going to examine that—" He hesitated for a word. "That brain-ectomy to see how it was done and how much skill it took."

He pointed his cigar at Turlogh. "You're going to have to be ready to lead an expedition to Pluto and show them where this Bubble City is."

"What about Gar?" asked Turlogh.

"His body will probably die under the examination he will be given. If not, and his brain is on Pluto, I doubt if the Plutonians will talk enough sense to enable us to risk saving him. For my money he's a goner." Mr. Foster saw the look on Turlogh's face and added, "I'm sorry."

Turlogh pulled himself together with a visible effort and shrugged his shoulders resignedly. "Well," he remarked, "Gar and I long ago talked it over and decided that if the time ever came when it was a choice between the safety of the Earth and our own lives, the Earth would come first."

He watched mutely as the two government men closed the door behind them. Then he called the airport to make reservations for the next plane back to Denver.

CHAPTER SIX

FOSTER quietly went to work when he got back to Washington, D.C. Even before he arrived he was busy getting things started via the plane's radio.

He had the report on the gadget in Gar's skull, and the experts' opinions on where the materials for more of the things could be bought. It was quite likely that Gar had brought several of those things concealed in his clothing, so that he would not have to depend on the resources of the Earth for more of them.

But investigation of everyone who had bought such materials in the past few days, and continued investigation of all who could buy them in the next few months would have to be made.

In addition there were the movements of Gar as he made his way from Denver to Chicago. They would have to be tracked down, he could have gone anyplace in the world on the way. His picture would have to be broadcast to every police station in the country and millions of officers would have to conduct almost a house to house inquiry. Many millions of people would look blankly at that picture and shake their heads and mutter, "No, I've never seen that guy before, or—wait a minute. No. No, that couldn't have been him."

It was almost a hopeless search. If they found any robots they could make sure by an x-ray. But by now there might be hundreds of them. It was entirely possible that the President might become a robot instrument of these beings on Pluto! His own men! Maybe even he might be made a robot.

Foster shuddered at the thought. No one would know the difference.

The whole picture of a race of sinister, diabolical intelligences, squatting in a hole on a planet millions of miles away while they quietly and patiently took over the Earth by a means that would be almost impossible to stop, was terrible to contemplate.

The *only* answer was to get at the core of the danger. Wipe them out! And he couldn't start the manufacture of atom bombs with just a phone call. Even the President couldn't start it. There would have to be a meeting of the world powers. All the evidence would have to be presented to them. There would be one or two stupid representatives who would suspect this as a subtle plan of the United States to get permission to make atom bombs so they could conquer the world! These men would have to be treated politely and their stupid arguments listened to while the whole planet was being threatened.

It could be that by the time the bombs were made the creatures on Pluto would be entrenched so strongly that they could prevent the takeoff of ships with atom bombs to Pluto! It would be impossible to subject every key figure in the world to daily x-rays to determine whether he had been made a robot or not.

Foster sighed wearily and wished that space travel had never come. The human race was just asking for trouble and had finally got it.

When the wheels of his plane touched the landing strip at the capitol he impatiently loosened the crash belt and was dropping off the wing of the plane almost before it came to a stop. A car was waiting to take him directly to the President. He had radioed ahead for the appointment so that not a minute would be lost.

And as he sank back in the rear seat of the car, he felt of the gun in the armpit holster under his coat. From now on he would not be able to trust *anybody*. At the least hint of danger he would have to shoot to kill. Even if the danger came from one of his own men!

GAR MOVED several of his robots to every side of his building so that he could keep an eye, or rather, a dozen eyes, on whatever might go on in Bubble City, and did some heavy thinking.

"There are two ways to look at this thing," he thought to himself. "Either Bubble City is so old that time means nothing, and every creature here spends most of his time doing nothing, or something is going on that probably smells."

Whatever might be going on, Gar decided he had better improve his position somewhat. He thought of a body exactly like his own as it had been, and willed it to be made. The machinery which occupied a good part of his building turned it out in a few hours.

Then he strutted around, feeling his old self again, while he watched himself through the eyes of his robot units. The novelty of seeing from many different positions at once had worn off. The marvel of the adaptability of the brain would never fade. His brain now had over two hundred independent visual centers which could work without interference with one another, or co-ordinate into a solid image in his mind when their visual ranges over lapped. He could do one thing with one body and another with another body, just as a man can read a book while walking, his legs doing work entirely unrelated to the work his eyes and hands are concentrated on.

Next he took one of his robots apart. It seemed to be made mostly of some sort of a plastic. The muscular system was interesting, but what he was most concerned with was the visual unit and the power unit.

The visual unit was complete by itself as he found out by taking it out of the robot and laying it on a bench, and still being able to see through the eyes.

The power unit worked something like the human heart, and was probably atom powered, since there seemed no source of power present. In the robots it pumped some fluid that probably was an alcohol, which powered the muscular system.

When taken out of the robot the fluid pumped out of it. Then the heart's rhythm increased until it shot a steady stream of air out of its exhaust port. It weighed perhaps three or four ounces.

The whole plan of the robot factory connected to his brain became clear. With most of the essential features of the robot bodies standardized, only the shape of a new robot, and the numbers of appendages would be variables in a new robot. The rest was standard just like the parts of machinery on Earth.

Gar wanted weapons of some sort. None of the parts of the robot looked promising, but they were all he had to work with. So he went to work.

In three days he had a thing about the size of a football that could move through the air, hover, turn, all at his mental command; that had eyes, ears, and a sharp heavy nose. It was powered by two robot hearts that sucked in the air in front and shot it out to the rear. Fins like those on fish did the steering.

As soon as he had perfected what he wanted he set his machinery to work and for the next few days it hummed steadily until he had thousands of his football robots stacked on the floors of the building.

Then he went on a real trip of exploration in half a dozen of them. None of the residents of Bubble City seemed to notice the small, oblong balls that glided among the buildings, so he explored everywhere, inside of the other buildings, and even the wall of the bubble.

Finally he stumbled across the tunnel at the bottom of the bubble. It was a smooth bore dropping at an angle of almost thirty degrees, perfectly straight as far as the eye could penetrate.

He sent the seeing eye balls, as he called them, speeding through the tunnel about a block apart. For hours they sped along. Finally, although there had been no change in the direction of the tube, it seemed to be going upward.

Gar puzzled over this and finally figured it out. On Earth, for example, if a tube could be bored from San Francisco to London in a perfectly straight line, a person entering it at San Francisco would coast downhill until he was half way through. The last half, beginning miles below the surface, would be all uphill. If the trip used up no energy in friction he would coast to a stop just at the surface in London.

"So this bore goes to one of the other warm areas!" Gar exclaimed to himself.

HIS DEDUCTION proved to be right. As the foremost ball reached the opening to the next bubble its eyes took in a sight even more awe inspiring than the first view of Bubble City itself.

There were no buildings here. It was a huge workshop. Thousands of atom powered motor generators were lined up on steps carved in the bottom half of the bubble. Thick copper bars led along these rows of generators, their ends leading finally to a gigantic unit in the center.

A floor that covered acres was crowded with huge cranes and machines, and an assembly line had been formed, on which rested over a hundred space ships partly completed.

Sub assembly lines were all over the place, Gar recognized many of the parts being made. What should he do?

He decided just to watch for the present. Up near the roof of the Bubble the wall seemed smooth. From vantage points up there he could take in all that went on below. He shot his floating balls out of the tunnel and upward. Then he backed them against the bubble roof where they stayed, held by the suction of the robot heart through its stern intake.

From half a dozen vantage points he studied what was going on. The huge thing in the middle of the floor of the cavern was an atom smasher. Through an opening on one side a thin but steady trickle of molten metal cascaded into a box of ingot molds. When one section filled, the box moved until the stream fell into the next mold.

No doubt by changing the raw material they could produce any element they had need for.

Where did the source of power come from? All this activity could not be the result of perpetual motion. There were millions of horsepower of energy flowing in the activity below. There must be some source of radioactive elements to provide such vast quantities of power.

Gar noticed that here and there were openings that led below the floor of the bubble. He determined to get below and see what there was. Over on one side of the floor there was a storage area where no one seemed to be moving.

He cut one of his seeing eyes loose from its position on the cavern roof and sailed toward this area. As he drew closer he saw that it was covered with piles of grey ingots of some kind of metal. He stopped and looked at one closely. The oxide coating on it was quite thick, indication that the ingots had probably lain untouched for a long time.

He wished he could pick one up, and regretted that he had not put small arms and hands on these floating robots so that he could get a sample of these ingots.

A hole gaped in the floor between two rows of ingots. He sank cautiously through it, ready to draw back at the first sign of movement below.

Underneath were more piles of the grey ingots. He floated cautiously along a corridor formed by two tiers of the ingots until he reached an open area.

Here he paused, looking around. Squat, muscular robots were monotonously picking up the ingots and sliding them through openings in a thing that looked like a gigantic furnace.

On the opposite side of the machine things that looked for all the world like bombs were emerging, and being carted to an elevator that led to the floor above. Atom bombs? The shape of the things indicated they were designed to drop through the atmosphere. The tail fins were shaped to produce a spin.

And the ships being built up above, coupled with these bombs, could spell only one word—war against Earth!

Gar knew the ban against atom bombs on Earth. He knew that even if Turlogh knew the truth about what had been taking place in Pluto he would not be able to convince the United Nations that they should get ready for an interplanetary war. And if the war were carried to Earth itself it would mean the end.

What were the Plutonians planning? Extermination of the Earthlings to keep any more from coming? Or conquest to enslave the race and rule the planet?

It didn't make much difference in the long run. From the number of bombs being turned out, the Earth would be blown to bits.

"I've got to stop this," he thought to himself. "I can't contact Earth. Or can I?"

The ships under construction up above! If he could steal one of those he might be able to get to Earth in time to warn them.

He let the floating ball come to rest on one of the piles of ingots, so that he could keep watching the production of the bombs, and concentrate his thoughts on the problem of bringing a robot into this bubble that could run a space ship. A floating robot with arms and legs might do the trick.

THE MAN stood in semi darkness staring at a white panel. Whenever he puffed on the cigarette hanging from his slack lips the flame at its end sent highlights of shadow over his features.

His eyes remained fixed on the white panel, and across it bobbed skulls complete with necks and part of the rib sections.

The man chuckled mirthlessly as one skull paused, its jaw moving up and down with a regular rhythm, then bobbed on until it disappeared to the right of the panel.

The next skull to enter the panel from the left had a strange dark area at the base of the skull. The man with the cigarette hastily pressed a button under his finger.

A loud voice suddenly began to shout somewhere. The sound entered the place where the man with the cigarette stood, but it was too muffled to make out words. The tone, however, was angry.

He grinned, but his eyes held a sick look. This was the third.

Near the other side of the panel several pairs of eyes also held a sick look. The eyes belonged to international police officers. And their hands held snub nosed automatics trained on the distinguished figure of Aaron Comstock, Canadian representative to the United Nations Court.

Mr. Comstock's naturally florid countenance was almost livid, and a steady stream of unquotable language was spilling from his thin lips, his hooked nose accenting the words by stabbing violently in whatever direction his head happened to point.

It pointed mostly at the two tight lipped men who were wrestling with his arms, trying to pin his wrists together with a pair of handcuffs. They finally succeeded in their efforts, and the distinguished Aaron Comstock was led through a door into a side room. A representative from the Soviet Union and one from France were seated on chairs against the wall, handcuffs adorning their wrists also.

In the middle of the room Foster was standing, nervously puffing on a black cigar, and gazing at the handcuffed men. Several men in the uniform of the international police stood about. Service automatics were prominently displayed on their left hips in shiny, brown leather holsters.

Behind a walnut desk at the far end of the room sat a heavy featured man, his short arms resting on the desk top. This was I.P. chief, Vladimir Dubrovski. His small eyes stared blankly across the room. His whole demeanor was that of a man patiently waiting.

"Five votes can kill the bill requesting permission to make atom bombs," Foster said suddenly. "There should be at least two more."

Dubrovski grunted, but said nothing.

During the next ten minutes three more figures were led into the room, handcuffed arms held by grim, uniformed men.

There were now sixty-seven robotized humans under custody altogether. The decision of the world court would without a doubt be in favor of making the bombs. There were more than enough space ships to carry them. But every day the personnel connected with every phase of the projected attack against Pluto would have to be viewed through a fluoroscope, and the guards themselves would also have to be examined.

The thing that was going on was too insidious. One of Foster's own men had left the headquarters building in Washington to go to the capitol building. He had arrived only ten minutes later than he should have. The fluoroscope showed the metal gadget at the base of his brain.

Attempts to remove the things by surgery had so far proven fatal. The attempt had only been made on two occasions. And there just weren't enough fluoroscopes available to do a complete job of surveillance. They were being taken by court order wherever they could be found, and factories were turning them out as fast as they could be manufactured; but an unknown number of robotized humans were undoubtedly running around loose. Enough to pose a real threat. And no doubt their numbers were growing steadily.

Experts were working on the two gadgets taken from their unfortunate, victims. So far they had not been able to learn the least thing about them.

FOSTER GLANCED at his watch. Two o'clock. The meeting would be starting. The desk phone rang, Dubrovski lifted it from its cradle and grunted. He listened for a few seconds and hung up. His small eyes held a humorous glint as his thick voice slurred out the words, "Quick work. They granted permission in twenty seconds by the stop watch of one of the reporters."

More developments came in later. The materials for the bombs were already stockpiled in various countries. Each nation would make its quota of bombs and load its own space ships. Guns from the international patrol fleet would be transferred to the space ships in the various factories under international surveillance. Once the work started it would only be a matter of a few days until the fleet could take off.

CHAPTER SEVEN

Turlogh gazed anxiously at the unconscious figure of Gar strapped to the bunk in his space ship. A middle aged doctor stood beside him.

"You think he'll be all right?" Turlogh asked.

"As right as he can be under the circumstances," the doctor reassured him. "It was Foster's idea to drug him and take him along. As soon as the drug wears off now we'll see how he is. You say he was rational and himself up to two days before you landed on Earth?"

"He seemed to be," Turlogh answered. He turned suddenly and went forward to the pilot room. Gazing through the side viewports he watched the rest of the fleet. The long, silver ships seemed to hang motionless in space. Rocket gasses shot from their stern tubes and vanished almost instantly behind them. Now and then a quick puff at the side of one of the ships would indicate the action of the steering rockets, correcting the course of a ship. Another day of the acceleration and their orbit for Pluto would be made. Then only the steering rockets would indicate that the fleet was anything more than a V-shaped formation of asteroids.

Turlogh relaxed the grim compression of his lips and lit a cigarette. He was more used to the long days of inactivity of space travel than the international police pilot at the controls. Years among the asteroids had given him the patience that only an interstellar traveler can attain.

Puffing contentedly on the cigarette, Turlogh looked through the eye piece of the ship telescope, changing its direction constantly and pressing studs that dropped or lifted filters that cut down the excessive light until the sky looked something like it did on Earth where the miles of atmosphere absorbed part of the rays.

His body swayed slightly as the automatic radar devices detected some small object ahead, plotted its course and altered the course of the ship just enough to avoid a collision. It swayed again as the course corrected itself, the object having flashed past too quickly for the eye to see.

The days wore on. The fleet passed the orbit of Mars before Gar regained consciousness. His mind was still a blank, but it might be possible that the alien beings on Pluto were passively spying through Gar's blankly staring eyes, and listening through his apparently deaf ears; so he was kept confined to his bunk, his wrists fastened to the bed with steel chains.

Turlogh spent most of his time at the telescope, peering ahead. Pluto became large enough to see. Imperceptibly it grew larger until it was a fair sized disc in the telescope.

GAR SET TO work designing a floating robot with arms and legs. After it was finished it would take hours to send it through the tunnel to the other bubble and it might be detected and all his careful spying brought to an immature end. If this happened he had his thousands of floating balls with hard noses kept in reserve. He would use these to do as much damage as he could.

What the Bubble City residents had in the way of counter measures he couldn't even begin to guess. The only one that he and Turlogh had ever talked with mentioned a period when they had fought over possession of the robots. No mention had been made of the kind of warfare they had engaged in, so there was no clue as to what they might do, or could do.

If he could get a few floating robots into the other bubble that could pick up things he could at least short out their banks of generators and perhaps burn up a few of them.

If he could wreck all their space ships except one, and get that for himself, he could force these beings to some sort of terms or destroy them, himself included.

Through the eyes of the floating balls in the other bubble he watched the progress of the work of making the space ships. A lull in the work on several of them enabled him to slip aboard and conceal himself in the shape of one of his seeing eye footballs over the instrument panel in the pilot room.

It amazed him how nearly like the ship he and Turlogh had come to Pluto in, these ships were. They might have been turned out by the same company back on Earth!

Finally the floating robot with arms and legs was finished. Gar sent it ahead at the same time putting his automatic machinery to work making dozens more of them. Powered with three hearts it shot into the tunnel and gained in speed until the cold light bulbs, spaced about fifty feet apart, became a blurred line of light.

It passed a long line of human shaped robots marching in single file through the tunnel. These were evidently to be the pilots of the ships! And surely they must have seen and heard him as he passed so closely over their heads. But if they did they gave no sign of it; and as the end of the tunnel came, and the eyes of this new robot sent to his brain the scene of activity and preparation for war, there was still no sign that any of the alien creatures whose brains rested in the tall, reed-like buildings in the other bubble were aware that he knew of their schemes.

Evidently they were quite human in that they could not see something they didn't expect. They had no robots that could sail through the air. They never looked up. And they seemed to be serenely ignoring him, thinking that since he had no more than they to work with he could be no threat to their plans.

Gar mentally shrugged his now almost forgotten shoulders. Perhaps he could be no threat to them. Perhaps they knew of everything he didn't just as people idly watch the antics of a kitten which grimly attacks a shoe, determined to bring the wearer of the shoe to the floor and claw him to bits. And perhaps they were just as amused at the things he was doing.

If that were the case—what difference did it make, so long as he could be free to put in the last lick? If they were underestimating him it would be their hard luck!

BUT GAR had a hunch that these beings, so incredibly old that all their mental habits were firmly fixed, had one track minds in spite of their thousands of focal centers of consciousness. He felt that once they had decided he could do no harm they had dismissed him from their thoughts. And since they were many, each one who saw his floating robots probably thought they were the work of one of themselves!

One thing that gave him this feeling was the fact that they did not seem to think of themselves as individuals. The one they had talked with had always said "we", never "I."

And in his own brief experience he had found that the focus of consciousness set up in his mind to direct and be aware through a single robot had a tendency to isolate itself from the rest of his mind completely, and communicate with other parts of his mind almost as a separate individual. Perhaps in time such focal centers would become individual minds, all within a single brain, each with its own individuality and desires.

He chuckled to himself. Goodness knows that the mind of an ordinary human often struggles with itself, trying to reach decisions between opposing desires. Suppose each desire of the mind could be carried out by a separate body!

As a result of all this thinking, Gar decided to be a little bolder. He now had floating robots the size of footballs, with two short arms and two telescoping legs, being completed at the rate of one every twenty minutes. As soon as one was finished he took control of it and sent it speeding through the tunnel to the other bubble. And as each one emerged at the other end it sped openly to one of the space ships and concealed itself above the instrument panel.

He even sent one into the ship that already had an armless and legless robot, and, since the ship was vacant at that moment, he greeted himself warmly.

"Hello, short, squat and ugly," he said with gay contempt through the new robot to the old one.

"Hello yourself," came from the seeing eye football. "I think you're cute with your football body, pointed nose, eyes and mouth like a goldfish, and arms and legs not much bigger around than straws in a soda fountain. I think if you ever get to Earth you could get a contract with the Disney Studios."

"Thenk yo," came the reply.

A moment later the pilot entered, followed by several robot mechanics. Then the ship began to move.

From his vantage points through the floating balls at the top of the bubble Gar watched the ships move slowly and one after another vanish into an opening in a side wall. Each ship had been built on a wheeled truck which could carry it to the surface for the takeoff.

The bore of this tunnel sloped upward at an angle of about ten degrees. At the top was a long airlock, freshly made, through which the ships passed, one at a time. On the outer surface of the planet the ships moved down a long roadway for a half a mile, then made a right angle turn and blasted off.

While this was going on Gar was in a mental quandary. He might have tried to gum up the works by taking over the first ship to enter the tunnel and somehow causing one of the bombs to explode, sealing the bubble. This might only have delayed the takeoff of the others. He might now take over one of the ships and bomb both bubbles, and if he succeeded he could destroy the Plutonian race completely.

Or he might take over all the ships at once and control the fleet. *But, could the Plutonians block out his control and substitute their own in his robots?* On the answer to that question hinged the success of anything he might try to do. *And he did not dare to take that risk.* Whatever he did must be final and irrevocable, and done without warning, so that any last minute attempts by the Plutonians to nullify his work would be impossible under any circumstances.

PLUTO HAD increased in size in the telescope until it was as large as the moon is to the naked eye on Earth when Turlogh saw the Plutonian ships take off. He radioed the commander of the fleet only to find that every ship was watching that takeoff.

But Turlogh could give information the other observers could not. He informed the commander that the ships were taking off from the second largest warm area on Pluto, while the Bubble City was under the largest of the three warm areas.

"Then no doubt both warm areas cover bubble cities," was the commander's conclusion.

"Perhaps the third one does, too," Turlogh added.

"Thank God we brought plenty of bombs," the commander said before signing off.

One after another of the sleek ships turned lazily on its axis and then spit gasses out of its stern tubes, to vanish in the distance. In two hours the ships were in battle formation, each a hundred miles from its nearest neighbor. Then, at a command from the flagship, the automatic fire switch on each ship was unlocked and pushed home.

Now anything that approached to within a hundred miles of any ship would be detected by the radar that ordinarily served merely to avoid collision with other objects. Its course would be plotted automatically just as before, but a small explosive bullet fired from one of the many guns, aimed automatically, would intercept the path of the object and hit it.

It was for that reason that each ship had to move out of the range of the others, and it was for that reason that the automatic fire switch was kept under lock, for if the switch were closed while the fleet was in close formation it might mean the end of the fleet. Each of the other ships would be detected and fired upon within six seconds after the switch was closed!

Such was the strength of the Earth fleet. Could the Plutonian fleet match it?

The commander in his flagship asked Turlogh that question over the radio.

"I don't know," answered Turlogh. "I only saw Bubble City, not the other place. There was no way that I could see that space ships could come from Bubble City. For all I know these Plutonians are old hands at space travel. If they are they probably have a few tricks up their sleeve that we don't know anything about. If they learned all they know from Gar they should be a cinch, because he never did know the first thing about radar. For that matter *I* couldn't tell how to build a completely automatic fire control mechanism."

"But they might have other tricks up their sleeves?" the commander persisted.

"They might," Turlogh replied. "Don't forget these ships ahead will be manned by robots. Self-preservation don't mean a thing to them. They may have robot torpedoes that can twist and turn on unpredictable paths; that can see where they're going and track us down. They undoubtedly can stand more acceleration than we can, and may be able to out maneuver us. In fact, they undoubtedly can! I would advise—" Turlogh hesitated.

"I see," the commander answered thoughtfully. "I realize your hesitancy, but the lives of all the men on just one ship are worth more than the life of a single man whose life is probably already forfeit."

"Yes, sir," Turlogh said dumbly.

At a radioed command the ships strung out and began a long arc out of the plane of the ecliptic to avoid the oncoming Plutonian fleet. The Plutonians guessed their maneuver and proved they were faster. Their ships spread out and went into a complex system of orbits around the planet which protected it nearly from any form of attack.

A bomb was launched experimentally by one of the Earth ships. When it reached the vicinity of the Plutonian net one of their ships emitted a cloud of white smoke. A few seconds later the heavens were lit up fiercely by the blast of the bomb. It had exploded harmlessly at least eight hundred miles from the surface of Pluto.

Half hour later six ships detached themselves from the Earth fleet and dived toward Pluto in close Indian file, their fire switches opened so that they could hold close together.

Turlogh watched, tightlipped, knowing that the men, in the lead ship at least, were committing deliberate suicide. Perhaps all of them would die in a vain effort to destroy the Plutonians.

He watched through the telescope as the six ships drew closer to the network of enemy space ships. The fate of two worlds hung in the balance.

Someone tapped him on the shoulder. It was the doctor.

"Gar has regained consciousness," the doctor said. "He is asking for you."

CHAPTER EIGHT

WHILE THE space ships were taking off from Pluto, Gar, through the eyes of the "cute" little football robots with legs and arms, perched above the instrument panels in the pilot rooms of the ships, watched what went on. He guessed from the actions of the crews and the movements of the ships that the Earth fleet had arrived.

He knew enough about the theory of space battle to guess that there would be feints on each side before the actual battle begun. So, keeping one corner of his mind turned on the ships, he directed most of his efforts toward trying something he had never dared to try before; "taking over" a robot of one of the Bubble City beings by force of will.

He didn't know quite how to go about it, but he had been studying the problem with what he had to go on. He had no trouble with his own robots. There was some subconscious "key" to each robot, so that his mind would contact it or sever connections with it at will.

"If I can isolate and bring to my conscious mind the factors that go into the problem of contacting a robot," he reasoned, "I should have it. It will be like a series of Yale locks, only instead of tumblers there will be thoughts. A series of thoughts that can take on a large number of combinations."

He thought this over and then went a step further. "If the thought necessary to contact any robot were mechanically induced by some external stimulus, and this stimulus was created by a thought, the whole thing would be simple. Each time a robot was turned out by my machinery, the key to contacting it would be hooked onto my brain, so that the association of the stimulus to the contact with the robot would be made automatically."

"Then," he exclaimed in triumph, "unless the series of keys in my makeup were known to the others they could not take over my robots or prevent me from holding my contact with them!"

He had another brilliant inspiration. Through the hundreds of football robots he had in reserve he began to search his building. In ten minutes he had located a room that held what he was looking for. Row upon row of small glass tubes were held in racks.

From each tube two fine wires led to a heavy conduit that went through the wall. The floating robot drifted along down the row. At the far end was a tube with its two fine wires broken! While the robot was looking along the row Gar had started a robot with flexible, delicate fingers toward the room. When it entered he lost no time in reconnecting the wires.

A thrill of exultation flashed through his brain. He was looking at the familiar hands of his Earth body. They were held in chains, but no matter. They were *his*. He lifted his eyes and saw a man he had never seen before. A thousand familiar feelings were crowding into his consciousness. He knew he was on a space ship. He looked carefully at the room and recognized a scratch on the frame of the hatchway. It was *his* ship.

The strange man was looking at him intently and his eyes held a look of fascination and fear.

"Is Turlogh on the ship?" Gar asked.

At the man's mute nod he said, "Get him. Get him at once. There's not a minute to lose."

THE MAN turned and fled from the room. A few seconds later Turlogh dashed through the opening. He took one look at Gar and saw the light of intelligence in his eyes. Then he exclaimed, "Gar! Is it really *you?*"

"Yes," Gar replied. "Forget the homecoming and tell me just what is happening now."

Turlogh told him in a few clipped sentences. He told him of the robotized humans on Earth, also, and started to tell him the details of the events leading up to the takeoff of the fleet when Gar stopped him.

"There's no time for that now," he said. "I've got to act fast." He lay back on the bunk to which he was chained and appeared to go to sleep. Turlogh spoke to him once and got no answer, so he sat down and waited. After a minute he stood up again and went back to the control room telescope to watch the drama going on.

The string of Earth ships was now within a few hundred miles of the range of the Plutonian ships. The telescope brought them up so that they seemed only a few city blocks distant.

A steering rocket on one of the Plutonian ships suddenly shot out hot gasses. The ship veered slightly. A ship to the right of it fired a shot.

The shot took the ship in the midsection, throwing out an eye searing flash of light. The two halves of the ship rolled over crazily as they fell away from each other.

The next minute the string of Earth ships shot through the area that had been covered by the wrecked ship. Their crews took no chances. Each ship, as it made sure it was through the net, dumped its load. They had aimed their thrust at such a point that if they got through they could do just that; dump their loads and be reasonably sure that they would hit the two largest warm spots. Then if they didn't get back they would not have died in vain.

When the lead ship dropped its load its radio technician yelled into the microphone, "Hurrah for Patrick Henry!" It later turned out that he was r. t. 1-c Henry Wong, called Sing Song by his buddies.

Each ship, as it dropped its load, braked into an orbit only a few miles above the surface of Pluto where the radar detectors from the enemy space ships could not pick them out easily.

The bombs, aggregating over six tons of the most efficient type of radioactive power, dropped lazily downward. They had split into two groups that separated farther and farther as they neared the planet.

A few minutes of careful measurement showed that they would make direct hits in the centers of the two largest warm areas, the largest would be hit in twenty-seven minutes, and the other in thirty-two.

Turlogh left the pilot room and went back to Gar. As he stepped through the doorway Gar looked up, a wan smile on his lips.

"Well, I did it," he said. His voice was calm. It sounded almost as if he welcomed what would come in less than half an hour.

"Yes," Turlogh's voice was vibrant with the hurt of the moment. He pulled two cigarettes out of a crumbled pack and stuck one in Gar's mouth. After he had lit both of them he sat on the edge of the bunk to which Gar was chained, wishing fervently that the keys to those chains were on board so that Gar could die a free man.

Both men were silent. Their eyes held a faraway look. Finally Gar said softly, "Remember that time in San Francisco, Turlogh?"

"Yeah," Turlogh answered gruffly. Then he grinned. "You never did tell me how you got your head stuck in the spittoon in the beer parlor."

GAR'S FACE turned red. "Believe it or not," he said, "I dropped a quarter in it and was trying to see where it was."

"Well I'll be damned," Turlogh murmured. "That's almost as bad as—" he stopped, his own face turning red.

"You mean the time you hid your money in a trash can in an alley so that no one could steal it from you while you were drunk, and then forgot which alley?" Gar asked.

"Yeah. Yeah," Turlogh grinned. "We were always a couple of dumb dodos. But I always thought I was the dumbest until now. Sticking your head in a spittoon to look for a quarter!" He snorted disgustedly.

"Well it wasn't just an ordinary quarter," Gar said. "I spent a lot of work on that one."

"Work?" Turlogh said. "What do you mean, work?"

"That quarter had two heads on it," Gar said with a knowing grin.

"Huh?" Turlogh exclaimed. A picture flashed into his mind of a quarter lying on a rubberized pavement by the side of a car in Bubble City, head side up, and Gar climbing out of the car to pick it up.

"Why you dirty—" He glared at Gar, then stopped. A muscle under his left eye twitched, and his jaw dropped downward in an agonized expression.

He wiped the expression off his face with the palm of his hand, leaving grief. A tear glistened in his eye as he turned his back on the figure of Gar, which lay quietly, its eyes staring blankly at the roof of the bunk.

At the door he turned and looked back. A pitying smile for that living body of a dead man softened his features. He muttered, "Son of a," as he left the room and went to the telescope.

He knew what he would see. And as he trained the telescope on what had been Bubble City he muttered softly to himself.

"What did you say, sir?" asked the officer who had relinquished the telescope to him.

"Huh?" asked Turlogh, taking his eye from the telescope to look at the officer. "Oh, I said, nuts."

"Oh," the officer said vaguely.

TURLOGH slopped beer on his shirt sleeve and on the bar as he angrily slapped his glass on the counter. "Go away," he said. "Don't bother me."

"Is your name Turlogh?" a feminine voice asked at his back.

"What's it to you," he growled. "Leave me alone."

"I ask you," she insisted. "Is your name Turlogh Hogan?"

"So what!" he said turning to face her.

"We have been looking for you for six months," she explained. "We want to make an expedition to Pluto and we've got to have you along."

"What do you want to go to Pluto for?" Turlogh said. "There's nothing there, Gar's dead."

"Just the same," she answered, "the government is forming an expedition to go to Pluto to explore the third warm area, and we need you along because you're the only one who has been on the surface."

"What do you need me for? I've never been in the third warm area, and the other two are destroyed along with my old pal Gar. Leave me alone. All I want to do is drink and forget it."

The girl didn't answer but turned and nodded imperceptibly to two men standing near the doorway of the beer parlor. These two men stepped forward, one on each side of Turlogh and lifted him forcibly from the stool.

"I'm afraid you'll have to go whether you want to or not," she said with a note of finality in her voice.

Turlogh's protests did not avail him as the two men pushed him along out of the beer parlor. Outside they shoved him into a car and followed him in, to sit on either side of him. The girl climbed in the front seat by the driver. In fifteen minutes Turlogh was standing in front of the desk of Port Commander Jensen of the North American Space Port just outside of Denver.

"I absolutely refuse to take any part in an expedition to Pluto," Turlogh said forcibly. He drove his fist toward the surface of the desk intending to put emphasis on his remark. His fist missed the desk by a foot and his chin followed it to land with a resounding thump on the edge of the desk. The Port Commander and the girl smiled quietly while Turlogh regained his feet and a certain amount of drunken composure.

"Maybe you don't understand why we are making this expedition," Commander Jensen said smoothly. "We have evidence which leads us to believe that Gar may still be alive. That's the reason we're forming this expedition."

"Gar! Alive!" exclaimed Turlogh.

"Oh, it's by no means certain," Jensen said, "but we believe it's entirely possible that he may still be alive in spite of the explosion, and whether he is or not, until I can know what is underneath that third warm area, we can never feel safe about Pluto."

The thought that Gar might still be alive sobered Turlogh instantly.

"I'll go," he said.

The girl and the Port Commander looked at each other and sighed with relief. "OK, get sobered up and pack," Jensen said, his voice now full of business and crisp. "The ships leave in twenty-four hours. If you need any money say so now because you have to be ready in twenty-four hours."

TURLOGH left the Port Commander's office his mind full of hope and anticipation of once more being out in space. He signaled a taxi, and when it pulled to a stop at the curb he climbed in.

When he turned to close the door the girl was crowding in after him, a mischievous smile on her face. "Hello," Turlogh exclaimed. "What are you tagging along for?"

"Just to make sure you don't go back to that beer parlor," she said.

"Oh," Turlogh grunted. He sat in silence while the taxi covered blocks. Occasionally his eyes stole in the direction of the girl. They turned stonily forward again when he saw that she was still watching him. Finally he said, "What's your name?"

"Frances Nichols," she said simply.

"Pleased ta meetcha," Turlogh grunted. Then he did a double take. "Are you any relation to Gar, my old partner?"

"I'm his baby sister," she said, the mischievous smile on her face again.

"Well I'll be damned," Turlogh said softly. "Gar never told me he had a sister. For that matter he never said anything about any of his folks, I guess maybe it was because I never asked him. Are you going along with us?"

"Yes," Frances replied. "As a matter of fact I'm the one who is responsible for this whole expedition. I can't believe that Gar is dead."

"What good would it do if he was still alive," Turlogh said hopelessly. "They've probably incinerated his body by now."

"No, they haven't," Frances said eagerly. "It's still alive and we are taking it along on this expedition."

"Oh," Turlogh grunted.

"Well, I don't think it will be much use," he went on. "I don't see how he could have survived that atom blast and if he survived the blast I don't see how he could survive the vacuum cold of space in the months since then. But if you think he's still alive that's good enough for me."

Suddenly he held out his hand, a warm grin on his space tanned face. Frances took it and they shook hands solemnly.

TURLOGH stood looking through the forward view screen at the enlarged disc of Pluto. To the right and to the left as far as the eye could reach an occasional silver flash showed the position of the other ships of the fleet. Similar flashes showed above the surface of Pluto indicating that the compact net of Plutonian ships still circled the planet.

"How are you going to get through those?" Turlogh asked the Captain who was intent on reports at his desk nearby.

"Our ships have picked up several thousand asteroids during the journey out here," he replied without looking up. "We are going to drop those in their screen and see if we can't exhaust their ammunition. At the same time we're going to try to bring a few of them down. Most of the fleet will remain out here. If we can get our ship and three or four others through their defense screen—that's all we want."

Turlogh's eyes again returned to the disc of Pluto and he watched it enlarge until it covered two-thirds of the forward screen.

Suddenly the right arm of the fleet phalanx began to move ahead. It swept majestically in a large circle in front of the rest of the fleet and from each of the ships several flashing objects broke loose to dive toward Pluto. They all reached the range of the Plutonian fleet's detectors at about the same time. The disc of Pluto lit up with thousands of flashes as the defense fleet went into action. Not a single asteroid of the thousands dropped by the Earth fleet got through. No sooner had the right wing of the fleet resumed its position than the left wing followed through in the same kind of maneuver. Once more the Plutonian defense destroyed the barrage.

"What now?" Turlogh asked the Captain.

"Oh, that was just a feint," the Captain replied. I wanted to see if their ships were still in working order without any directing intelligence to keep them going. To get through is really a matter of figuring out the mathematics of their defensive maneuvers."

Several hours later the warning gong sounded and the ship Turlogh was on suddenly accelerated in a full power dive toward the surface of Pluto. Almost before the power dive had begun the ship was straightening out a few thousand feet above Pluto's surface and the landscape was beginning to slow its mad flight across the view screen. They were through!

The landscape below sped by at the rate of 3,000 miles an hour. Bleak mountain crags were succeeded by black bottomless abysses in rapid succession. The huge hole which had once been Bubble City loomed briefly and was left behind.

A few spurts from the steering rockets set the course of the ship toward the only remaining warm area. This area flashed by underneath the ship an hour later.

Then began the routine work of stabilizing the ship's orbit and feeding data to the landing robot that would set them safely on the surface when they once again circled the planet.

Turlogh remembered the strange dreams he had had that first time while his and Gar's ship circled the planet while they were surveying it. He wondered if there were any intelligences left in Bubble City which could reach out and probe their minds.

The ship lashed abruptly into the night side on the airless planet. A few moments later the Captain rose.

"Well," he explained, "I don't think there's anything to do now but wait. Let's have a little something to eat, and then maybe we can have a bridge game afterwards if you feel like it."

TEN HOURS later, after a seemingly uneventful night, the ship ground to a stop and Turlogh unstrapped himself from his shock seat. He had to help Frances into her space suit.

She confessed excitedly that she had never been to any of the other planets before. Her aloofness at the beginning of the trip was disappearing rapidly.

By the time he and Frances were ready to leave the ship, several of the crew had passed through the airlock and could be seen standing in the frozen snow of solidified atmosphere that covered the surface outside.

"Is that really frozen air?" Frances asked excitedly. "Or is it just snow?"

"That's air, not mere snow." Turlogh said. "Before Bubble City was exploded, the dwellers used to send robots out to shovel it into cars where it was taken inside Bubble City to replenish their atmosphere. The sun is so far away from Pluto that even the full force of its rays isn't sufficient to melt the frozen atmosphere that covers most of its surface."

"Won't we freeze to death standing in it?" Frances asked.

"You won't even feel it," Turlogh replied. "Your suit has an automatic heating system which keeps its inner surface at just the right heat for you to be comfortable regardless of what it is outside."

The bloated arm of Turlogh's suit motioned toward the airlock inviting Frances to precede him. She hung back.

"I—I'm scared," she said nervously.

"Go ahead," Turlogh replied. "There's nothing to be afraid of."

Soon they were standing on the surface outside with those of the crew who had gone out before. The Captain's voice sounded in Turlogh's ear phones.

"Would you have any idea," it said, "where we might find an entrance to this bubble?"

"No, I don't," Turlogh answered. "We'll just have to hunt around and see if we can find an entrance. There should be several if this bubble is like the other two were. If we can't find an entrance we'll have to go to the other two bubbles and try to find an underground connection that leads to this one."

"We'd better all spread out and look then," the Captain's voice said.

"Everybody be careful," Turlogh warned. "The rock surface under this frozen snow is sharp and brittle. If you fall your suit is liable to be cut open on the sharp edges, and you all know what that means."

"Yes," the Captain's voice cut in. "I don't want any casualties through carelessness."

TWO HOURS later the bloated figures of the explorers dragged back toward the ship. One by one they advanced through the airlock until all were gathered once more inside the ship.

As each one discarded his suit he shook his head indicating that he had found nothing. As the last figure climbed in and reported his failure the Captain shrugged his shoulders resignedly.

"I guess we'll have to go to Bubble City and try to find a subterranean tunnel leading toward this section."

"Does that mean that we'll have to climb over mountains and travel on foot to Bubble City?" Frances asked.

"Certainly not," the Captain replied. "We'll just take off, establish an orbit, and go through the same process we did to land here, but land near Bubble City instead. Everyone to your station. We takeoff at once."

CHAPTER NINE

Turlogh sat on the edge of the gaping hole in Pluto that exposed what had once been Bubble City. His eyes swept downward taking in the wreckage of the reed-like skyscrapers that had once climbed thousands of feet from the floor of the bubble to its ceiling.

These buildings were now broken and twisted, the roof of the bubble fallen. Huge boulders perched on the wreckage of the skyscrapers below.

Turlogh's eyes held a hopeless look. How could they find Gar in all that wreckage when every building had looked like every other building? Unless there were some way Gar's brain could communicate with them it would be a hopeless task, Gar's body in the space ship had shown no response— no indication as to whether Gar still lived or not.

Frances crept up to stand silently by Turlogh and look with awe at the wreckage left by the atom bombs which had been dropped to destroy the threat to civilization embodied in those intelligent skyscrapers whose multifaceted minds could direct any number of robot creatures of all descriptions. The voice of the Captain sounded in Turlogh's earphones.

"Where can we get down into the bubble?" he asked.

"I'll show you," Turlogh said, turning.

He led the way to the doorway through which he and Gar had gone what seemed centuries ago. Inside things were just the way he had left them. Even the car still sat silently on the plastic road bed.

With Turlogh leading the way and Frances marching by his side the bloated figures in space suits walked down the spiraling incline which wound through solid rock to the bottom of the bubble.

When they came to the exit of the tunnel Turlogh pulled up in despair. The fragile roadway which had once spanned the gulf from the wall of the bubble to the nearest skyscraper was gone. Where it had been was only empty space which dropped abruptly to the depths below.

The Captain strode forward and took in the situation at a glance.

"Is this the only entrance you know to the bubble?" he asked, turning to Turlogh.

"Yes," Turlogh answered, hopelessly.

"Well," the Captain replied, "that means we have to figure out some way to get down to the bottom from here."

Turlogh surveyed the wreckage that spread out below. The reed-like skyscrapers were jammed together like broken match sticks.

Looking through his powerful Army binoculars he studied detail after detail, hoping to find some evidence that life still existed in these ruins.

SUDDENLY a startled exclamation broke from his lips. His binoculars settled on one spot near the far edge of the bubble. He had seen a movement there. As he brought the spot into sharp focus he saw a strange creature which stood, statue-like, its head turned toward the party of Earthmen.

Then, as if sensing it had been discovered, it turned and disappeared from sight behind a broken piece of masonry.

"Hey," Turlogh exclaimed, "I just saw something."

"What was it?" Frances asked.

"Did it move?" asked the Captain.

"I don't know what it was," Turlogh said. "It disappeared before I could take in its details, but it didn't look like any kind of animal I've ever seen before. Whatever it was it wasn't wearing a space suit, so it must have been a mechanical robot."

"That means we had better be careful," the Captain said. "If there is any kind of intelligence left in these ruins it will probably be out to get revenge for what we did when we were here before."

He turned to his men and issued a few brief orders.

Two hours later the men returned from the ship with two portable space cannon and a winch. The cannon and winch were set up on the lip of the cliff and soon the winch was dropping space-suited figures to the floor of the bubble below.

"From here on you're the boss," the Captain said to Turlogh. "You know more of the layout of Bubble City and where we might find a tunnel leading to the third warm area than we do, and also, you know more of what we might be getting into. We'll follow your orders without question."

"I think what we better do first," Turlogh said, "is try to get through the wreckage to the spot where I saw that creature just now."

"That's a good idea," the Captain said, "let's go."

The floor of Bubble City was fairly free of wreckage. The buildings in falling had jammed tightly together far above the lower levels and formed a barrier which stopped the plunging rocks from the shattered top of the bubble. Here and there lay bits of smashed machinery and unearthly figures which had once been the mechanical robots controlled by the minds in the skyscrapers. Now they lay motionless where they had been when the atom bomb plunged through the roof of the bubble to destroy the civilization that had lain hidden there for millions of years.

Frances stayed close to Turlogh asking innumerable questions about everything they passed. A line of robot street sweepers stood untouched by the fallen debris which had miraculously missed them. A spider legged creature whose function could not be determined from its appearance lay crumpled, a huge boulder having landed a direct hit. Here and there white tinges of frozen air covered the street and the objects they passed as they made their way slowly across the ruined city.

"The tunnel to the second bubble," Turlogh explained to the Captain, "left this bubble on the side that is in direct line with that bubble, so I think that we stand our best chance of finding a tunnel to the third bubble by going to the side of the city facing in that direction."

"That's the direction in which you saw the thing that vanished when we were standing up on the cliff, isn't it?" the Captain asked.

"Yes," Turlogh exclaimed, "I have a hunch he came from the third bubble."

"You say he didn't have a space suit on?" Frances asked.

"It didn't look like a space suit," Turlogh replied, "but with such fantastic creatures around it could just as well have been the space suit I saw with something unknown inside it."

AFTER TWO hours of slow trudging, the far wall of the bubble could be seen down the length of the street they were on. The Captain ordered the men to be on the alert. Electron guns were drawn and the men imperceptibly formed a protective circle around the Captain, Frances, and Turlogh.

Without warning, bodies began to rain down on the group, bowling the men over before they could bring their electron guns into play, Turlogh rolled in his fall, landing on his feet in time to blast one of the creatures which swarmed among them.

As swiftly as they had come, the creatures bounded into the air and vanished in the wreckage above.

To Turlogh's dazed ears came the cry of Frances calling for help. Desperately he looked around. Frances was gone!

A swift count showed that no one else was missing and no one had been hurt in the attack except the creature that Turlogh had shot. The swift, desperate attempt at pursuit ended in futility. There was no trace of the attackers or sign of which way they had fled.

Turlogh and the Captain examined curiously the body of the strange creature. It was shaped something like a strange insect.

Its short, squat body was held up by eight, pipe stem legs, the rear four of which were much longer than the front four, evidently for the purposes of jumping.

At the front end of the body a smaller body rose straight up. To this were attached eight fragile looking arms which ended in long, flexible, finger-like tendrils. This smaller body was topped by a head that looked more like the bud of a giant Astor than anything else. The skin of the creature was hard and woody, a dark blue green in color.

"Let's get going," Turlogh ground out impatiently. "We've got to get to the tunnel entrance before they do or there's no telling what we'll get into before we can rescue Frances."

Without waiting to see what the others would do, Turlogh broke into a clumsy trot cursing the space suit which held him back.

He reached the wall of the bubble and saw a dark opening looming a hundred feet to his right. As he looked, several bounding figures dashed into the opening. Two of them were carrying the space-suited figure of Frances between them.

With his breath tearing at his lungs in agonized sobs, Turlogh dashed after them, hesitating at the mouth of the tunnel only long enough to be sure the Captain and his men had seen him go into it. The tunnel slanted sharply downward.

Turlogh braked to a stop. If this tunnel led to the third bubble and continued in a straight line through the planet, there would be a long hard climb at the other end. If they could find some kind of a car which could coast along the smooth floor of the tunnel, its momentum would carry it most of the way so that any time lost in looking for a conveyance would be more than made up by the speed with which they could travel.

He spoke through his microphone telling the Captain of this plan. At once the Captain and the men spread out to look for the nearest of the several cars they had seen setting idly along the roadway.

While Turlogh waited he tried desperately to contact Frances through his radio but got no answer.

One of the men discovered a shed a short distance from the mouth of the tunnel in which were cars designed to travel through the tunnel. He called for help and soon a car was poised at the tunnel's mouth ready for the journey into the heart of the planet which Turlogh fervently hoped would lead safely to the third bubble.

AS THE car gathered momentum it seemed to threaten to pull the men loose from their precarious perches on its surface. Darkness was absolute. The car bounced from one side of the tunnel to another, rider wheels on its sides fending the car off from the walls which rushed madly by. Hour after hour the car gained in speed until finally an imperceptible shift in acceleration told the men that the long upward path toward the surface had begun.

Turlogh peered ahead through the stygian gloom fearful that the car would overtake the fleeing creatures and plow into them, killing Frances along with them. As the car began to gradually slow down on its upward climb Turlogh began to wonder if they had taken Frances along this tunnel. Unless they had had a car hidden a short ways down in the tunnel they should have been overtaken long ago.

There was no way of stopping, however, and if there had been, the momentum gained on the long downward trip would have to be supplanted by slow and tedious muscular exertion. It would be better to let the car coast to a stop and explore. If no trace of Frances and her captors could be found, then they could come back the same way they had gone in less time than it would take for them to walk. Finally the Captain broke the long silence.

"In our haste," he said, "we forgot about air. We don't have enough oxygen left in our tanks to get back to the ship even if we could turn around right this minute and go back as fast as we have come."

A desperate gloom settled over the company of men. Whether they found Frances or not there was no hope.

Suddenly the car gave a slight lurch forward and a faint vibration could be felt through its floor.

"There must be power at this end anyway," Turlogh exclaimed.

"Everybody ready for combat," the Captain ordered. The grim-faced men clung to the handholds on the car ready to spring off at a moment's notice of an airlock directly ahead. The car slid sickenly to a stop just beyond the airlock. Turlogh leaped to the ground, his electron gun held ready to blast anything that moved.

AHEAD loomed the vastness of the gigantic interior of the third bubble. No skyscrapers reared their stem-like structures toward the ceiling of this hollow sphere. Instead, acre upon acre of dense vegetation covered the floor. Above, a dazzling glow seemed to emanate from the roof with light that might have come from the sun.

Here and there through the vegetation could be seen creatures similar to that that Turlogh had blasted with his electron gun, scurrying ant-like in purposeless haste. None of them seemed to be aware of the arrival of the men. One near at hand paused before a leafy bush. Buds protruded from the bush in all directions, exactly the same in appearance as the buds that topped the insect-like bodies of the creatures. The creature who had paused bent forward, its bud-like head opening, the petals spreading out as if it were about to bloom. A bud on the plant opened in the same fashion. The two opened buds came together and closed to form a tight knot. Creature and plant remained motionless.

Full of curiosity, the men advanced until they stood behind this strange union of plant and animal. The knot that joined the two was vibrating rapidly.

"What goes on?" one of the men exclaimed. No one answered him.

A noise sounded at the back of the group. The men turned.

Hundreds of the creatures had crept up on them from behind. They were now advancing slowly, their flower-like heads open and fluctuating hostilely. As a unit the men pressed the studs on their electron guns and cursed desperately when no lethal beam of electrons blasted forth.

"Atmosphere," groaned Turlogh.

The men reached for their automatics. These blasted forth with deafening sound moving down the first wave of attackers. They were replaced instantly by others who rushed forward, blindly oblivious of the destruction that met them.

Turlogh unloosed the catch on his plexi-glass helmet and pushed it back so that it rested on the back of his suit, leaving his head free. He gulped refreshing drafts of cool, flower-scented air.

The waves of creatures were getting closer and closer before they were mowed down. They were now attacking from all directions, and the men formed a compact circle.

It couldn't last. There was no time to reload. With alien bodies piled four deep in front of them, the men were engulfed by a wave of the sweet-smelling insect-like monstrosities.

Turlogh felt something cloyingly sweet spread over his face. He opened his mouth to breathe. The syrupy stuff choked him. His senses swirled and he lost consciousness.

WHEN Frances felt herself borne into the air she cried out in alarm. Her senses reeled as broken spires and fragments of the bubble buildings rushed by her in insane lurches. Little by little she became aware of the creatures that were carrying her.

A few moments later she saw the dark opening of a tunnel in the bubble wall loom briefly before her. Then darkness swept past her and her only awareness was of her sickening rise and fall from the grasshopper-like leaps of her captors.

After what seemed like centuries this stopped. She was laying on the floor and throughout her suit she felt the vibration of something approaching. The vibration rose in rapid crescendo to a peak and then descended the scale once more. She sensed that some rapidly moving object had passed in the tunnel.

The monotonous, jumping advance was again taken up. The rhythm of the slow leaps lulled her weary senses until at last she fell asleep.

How long she remained asleep she had no way of knowing. She was awakened by a blinding glare that hurt her eyes. She opened them to see a vast expanse of space which ended against a curving wall miles away over the top of a forest of dense vegetation.

The creatures that carried her did not stop. She saw the empty car just outside the tunnel opening and stared uncomprehendingly at the pile of bodies of creatures similar to her captor.

Something fumbled at the throat of her suit and her transparent helmet was thrown back. The sweet scented air entered her lungs with refreshing exhilaration. It was not until then that she realized the oxygen in her tanks was nearly exhausted.

She glanced curiously at her nearest captor. He looked to her like a giant katydid with a flower bud for a head. His grasshopper-like leaps had ceased and he was now trotting smoothly toward the fringe of the forest of vegetation.

Frances breathed deeply, preparing herself for an attempt at freedom. Her captors entered the forest and the blazing ceiling of the bubble was lost to view above the overhead limb and leaves.

The plants seemed to be all of the same kind; thick, trunk-like stalks rising briefly to merge into gigantic, foot thick leaves that spread their huge surfaces to catch every ray from the blazing, radioactive light above.

Short spikes radiated out from a bulbous mass at the heart of each plant. At the end of each spike was a bud that looked about to burst into bloom.

Frances was carried along deeper and deeper into this forest of strange plants. At last her captors came to a stop and circled one of the growths that seemed larger than the others. The buds on the radiating stalks of this plant opened wide exposing bright red maws with honey-combed surfaces. One of the creatures stepped forward for the first time. Frances noticed that the bud that topped its body had also opened. The two buds came together and their membranous coverings intertwined to form them into a single ball. To all appearances the insect-like animal was now part and parcel of the plant itself.

Breathless with amazement Frances could do nothing more than watch as one after another of the group that had captured her joined itself to the plant. Plant and animals seemed to have forgotten her. Clumsily she ran away through the gloomy corridors, her space suit retarding her progress until the nightmarish scene was lost to view.

She had no idea where she might go to escape. She was completely lost. The landscape gave no clue as to which way she should turn to retrace her steps back to the tunnel. Panic clutched at her brain sending its nightmarish tendrils to her pounding heart. She wanted to scream and cry for help.

One of the strange creatures dashed by immediately in front of her taking no notice of her. She plunged madly forward not daring to stop, not knowing where she was going, until, completely exhausted, she dropped into the sandy loam and gave way to despair.

CHAPTER TEN

TURLOGH'S senses returned slowly. He tried to move but could feel not the slightest sensation from his body. He felt as if he were a disembodied mind aware of his surroundings but with no material vehicle to obey his will. His eyes blinked every few seconds but he knew this only because of the momentary blotting out of his vision, not from any feeling the movement of his eyelids imparted to his brain. There was not even a numb sensation, not the slightest feeling of any kind came from his body.

Strange thoughts seemed to impinge themselves upon his consciousness as his interest in his efforts to make contact with his body waned. His attention turned to these thoughts.

They seemed to be strange—alien, but as he concentrated they began to take on meaning. They seemed to be the thoughts of dozens of creatures around him, invisible to his eyes. His eyes could see nothing but the sandy loam that formed the floor of this vast forest, and the monstrous plants with their huge bulbous growth, their trunk-like stems topped by thick meaty looking leaves and their short flower stalks, radiating like spokes from the bulbous mass. Turlogh's now alert consciousness began to piece together connected fragments of thoughts.

Except for their strangeness he might have believed them his own thoughts. There seemed to be a general discussion going on concerning the arrival of the Earthmen. There was a pause. Then the thought came, "Turlogh is awake."

"Who are you?" Turlogh asked in his mind.

"I, or we, are the mind of Pluto."

"Where are you?" Turlogh asked.

"We are everyplace and no place," came the reply. "Physically we are embodied in the plants of this forest and the creatures, but actually we are not because the death of any of them does not alter our thoughts nor can any of them think as an independent entity. We are one and yet several."

"Are you the mind of the skyscrapers?" Turlogh asked.

"No," came the emphatic denial, "that was separate."

"What are you going to do to us now that you've got us?" asked Turlogh.

"That remains to be seen," came the reply. "If you come in peace you can go in peace. If you come to destroy as you did once before you will be destroyed."

"I suppose that you've got my brain out like you have Gar's," Turlogh said. "I can't feel anything. All I can do is think."

"No we haven't," came the reply. "In a short while now all your faculties will return. You're just under the influence of a drug whose effects will wear off."

Turlogh thought this over. "Why did you kidnap Frances?" he asked.

"We wanted you to come here," was the reply, "and reading your mind we knew that you would be certain to follow if we brought her forcibly."

"Where is she now?" Turlogh demanded.

"She's here," came the enigmatical reply.

Turlogh grunted. Then startled realization came that he had actually grunted. His senses were returning. He could hear physical sounds now. The slither-slither of the bubble creatures dashing over the ground in their senseless pursuits and an almost imperceptible rustle of the foliage of the plants around him.

"Is Gar still alive?" he said.

"The one you call Gar," came the reply, "is one of the few still alive in Bubble City. He is helpless but kept alive by the radioactive heat of his protective case."

NOW TURLOGH could feel the blood forcing through his veins and the sharp particles of sand against the palms of his hands where they dug into the soil.

He opened his eyes and stood up weakly. After a few staggering steps he felt his strength return.

The others of the party lay in various positions around him still unconscious. While he waited for consciousness to return to them he examined one of the strange plants.

A half dozen of the Plutonian creatures were attached to it. With a whistle of amazement he noticed that there were numerous small shoots growing out from the central mass to which were attached miniature additions of the full grown Plutonians. On its smaller stalks were round pods which from their translucent appearance seemed to be fresh growths. This then was the way the Plutonians came into existence. The plants of this forest were a curious combination of plant and animal life. The Plutonians were the animal fruit of the plant. Turlogh could now see the natural evolution of this animal-plant race as it developed into a skyscraper civilization of multifaceted minds controlling mechanical robots in the same manner that they controlled the naturally grown animal creatures.

Somewhere along the line of the past a mechanical civilization had begun which eventually broke off from the parent mind and became a separate entity, Turlogh examined one of the full-grown animals attached to the nearest plant.

"Why does it have to attach itself?" he asked.

"For nourishment and to impart information," came the reply.

As if in response to his unspoken request the entwined wrappings of the connection between the creature and the plant rolled back and the connection broke with a soft sucking sound. Turlogh looked into the red maw of the creature and saw that it was moist. Droplets of a greenish fluid were forming on its red surface. Evidently the fluid passed from plant to animal and back again through the thin walls by osmotic pressure. The Plutonians were neither plant nor animal but a mixture of both.

The creature again joined itself to the plant. It reminded Turlogh of a calf nursing. He chuckled mirthlessly to himself.

The other men were now stirring. One by one they opened their eyes and stood up swaying until they regained their strength. The effects of the drug seemed to wear off as quickly as it had taken hold and there were no after effects. The Captain rubbed his forehead dazedly. "That's funny," he said. "I could have sworn I was talking to somebody just before I woke up."

"You were," Turlogh said with a grin, "you were talking to this," and he made a motion with his hand to include the forest around them.

"You mean that?" the Captain asked in amazement.

"Yes," Turlogh said crisply. "This forest has an intelligent mind just like the one we destroyed in Bubble City except that it has no mechanical civilization. This mass mind is embodied in those bulbous growths that form the hearts of the plants."

The Captain opened his mouth.

"Careful what you say," Turlogh said sharply, "the mass mind of this forest can read your thoughts." Then he closed his eyes and thought, "Take us to Frances."

"No," came the reply. "If we take you to Frances you will leave, and you must stay until we are sure what you intend doing."

TURLOGH told the Captain and the men what the Plutonian mind had just said. The Captain compressed his lips grimly.

"You say the brains of this mind are embodied in the bulbous centers of these plants?" he asked Turlogh. Turlogh closed his eyes and relayed the question.

"Yes," came the answer.

"Very well then," the Captain said, "tell this creature we'll start putting slugs in every bulbous mass around here until it consents to lead us to Frances."

Nothing but silence met this challenge. The Captain waited belligerently with his gun drawn.

Finally he pointed it at the heart of one of the plants and pulled the trigger. The plant shuddered convulsively and the creatures attached to it loosed themselves and ran off in panic. The Captain let his gun drop half ashamed of his act.

"I wonder what they'll do?" he whispered.

As if in reply, Frances appeared stumbling as she walked toward them. Her eyes, reddened from weeping, showed their relief at her having found them.

Turlogh rushed forward to meet her. As he put his hands forward to embrace her she vanished.

A soft laughter swept around the men and the rustling of the plants increased. "There's our reply," came a voice in the mind of Turlogh.

The Captain cursed under his breath and sent shots into three more of the plants. The first plant was curiously shriveling up. The thick fluid was flowing from the gapping bullet hole on to the sandy loam.

"Stop," the voice cried in Turlogh's mind. He signaled the Captain to stop firing. Then the voice went on.

"You cannot possibly destroy all of me. If just one of the plants remains alive I will still exist. If you agree to leave

Pluto and never come back I will return Frances to you and allow you to go unharmed. If you don't I will send my creatures against you once more."

"How do we know," Turlogh asked, "that you won't try the same thing that Bubble City did? After all we are a civilization too, and as long as we think you are a threat we will try to destroy you. If you kill us the fleet will blow up your bubble and destroy you before they go back to Earth."

"We have no desire for conquest," came the reply. "We are the ones who chose to remain aloof from a mechanical development."

"What's the use of arguing with it," one of the men said despairingly, "we haven't got enough oxygen to get back to the ship anyway. Let's start a fire and burn down the whole shootin' match."

A wave of terror blasted onto Turlogh's mind from the plants.

"Ha," the Captain exclaimed, "so it's afraid of fire." A familiar voice swept into Turlogh's mind.

"Is that you Turlogh?" it asked.

"Gar!" Turlogh exclaimed with a glad cry.

"Yes, Turlogh," came Gar's reply.

"Where are you? Turlogh asked.

"I don't know," Gar replied, "but don't do any more damage. The mind of the forest is not like the mind of Bubble City. It's honest and peaceful. It knows where I am but can't do anything to help me, but if you agree not to destroy the forest they will show you where I am and will help you get me off the planet."

"Can you contact your body in the space ship?" asked Turlogh.

"No," Gar replied. "The physical connections are broken, but they can be restored."

"If you will agree to leave in peace," came the thoughts of the forest, "we will return Frances to you and show you where Gar is."

"What do you think?" Turlogh asked the Captain.

"Well," said the Captain, "I guess we can take precautions to keep the forest from ever being a threat to the Earth. We can set up our own screen around Pluto to blast anything that leaves Pluto's surface."

"Do we agree then?" Turlogh asked.

"Sure, go ahead," the Captain said.

"One of my creatures will lead you to Frances," came the voice of the forest.

ONE of the Plutonians detached himself from a nearby plant and started off through the forest. The men followed. After half an hour of wandering they saw Frances ahead.

She saw them at the same time and broke into a trot running toward them, Turlogh dashed to meet her and threw his arms around her bloated space suit, kissing her before she had time to protest. This time she didn't vanish. She was real.

The creature that had led them to Frances turned and started off in a different direction. They followed him. Soon they came to the edge of the forest where it grew up almost to the wall of the bubble. A spring of steaming fluid trickled from a small opening in the wall. Before it reached the ground it evaporated. A blast of frigid air seemed to come from this spring.

"This is liquid air," came the voice of the forest. "You may replenish your oxygen tanks here."

"Oh, boy," one of the men exclaimed, "maybe we'll live through this yet."

The men began unstrapping one another's oxygen tanks. The suit connection to the tank was a short elbow which reached the tank at right angles. One after another the tanks were held under the stream of liquid air until they were full.

When the last tank had been strapped back into place the Plutonian started off following the curvature of the bubble wall at the fringe of the forest. Half an hour later the car upon which the men had ridden from Bubble City came into sight. The men piled on to the car, with Turlogh and the Captain lifting Frances to a safe position on it. The Plutonian also hopped on and then the car started with a slight hum. The long journey back to Bubble City had begun.

Several hours later in the blackness of the tunnel the car drifted to a stop, its momentum exhausted. Quickly the men leaped off before it began its return to the third bubble.

The Plutonian stoically started up the steep incline. They followed. Before they had gone very far, a white disk of light appeared in the distance ahead of them. It was the end of the tunnel.

The Plutonian reached it ahead of them and stood waiting until they could catch up, then he started off through the wreckage.

At last he stopped before an entrance in the base of what had once been one of the giant skyscrapers. Then he led the group to this building and to a doorway which led into an inner room. He stepped aside. Turlogh pushed past him into a small square room with a low ceiling.

On a pedestal in the exact center of this room was a transparent sphere in which a cloudy vapor swirled lazily. Floating in this vapor or liquid was a human brain, a flexible tube leading from down to the pedestal upon which the sphere rested.

"So you got here at last," Turlogh heard Gar's voice in his mind.

"My, how you've changed since the last time I saw you," Turlogh said, grinning.

"Oh it's not so bad," Gar replied. "I'm used to it now."

"Can you see us?" Turlogh asked.

"Vaguely," Gar replied.

"How the heck are we going to get him out of here?" the Captain burst in.

"There's only one way you could do it," Gar's voice sounded in Turlogh's brain. "It would be impossible to take my brain out of this sphere without killing it. You will have to take me, sphere and all, or leave me where I am."

"Turlogh," Gar's mind continued, "the robot control room is just above this. The connections from my brain down through this pedestal hook on to a cable which leads to that room.

Either there's a break someplace or, what is more likely, the power source is gone. If you can find the trouble I have a robot on each of those space ships circling the planet. With my robot controls restored I can make all of those ships destroy each other."

Turlogh relayed the information to the Captain. "That means we'll have to get a technician down from the ship," the Captain said. "Maybe he can find the power source and restore it."

CHAPTER ELEVEN

TWO WEEKS later the winch on the edge of the cliff, now transformed into a full-fledged derrick, slowly lifted a large packing case from the floor of Bubble City. It swung lazily as it rose higher and higher. Perched on the top of the case were space-suited figures with long poles to fend the box away from the sides of the cliff.

When it came even with the winch it was pulled carefully inward and dropped on to a car. Three jeeps hooked to the car pulled the packing case up the steep spiraling incline to the surface and out into the snow of frozen air crystals to the cargo port of the space ship. In this packing box was the brain of Gar in its transparent sphere, and the robot control banks. Frances and Turlogh followed the truck anxiously. At last the packing case was slid over through the port into the ship's storeroom. When the port cover clanged shut, Frances heaved a sigh of relief.

"That's over," she exclaimed, "I was so afraid the cable would break when they lifted him, or the truck would tip over. Now everything's all right and we can take him back to Earth where he can live a normal life again—I hope."

One by one the space-suited figures entered the ship and climbed out of their suits. An hour later with a blast of rocket jets that sent steamy clouds shooting for miles behind them, the space ship took off, followed in rapid succession by the other ships. Faster and faster, until the curvature of Pluto's surface could be seen through the view ports.

Far above, the silver flashes of Pluto's defense screen of space ships could be seen. They were no threat from below as they were set to fire only on approaching objects from above. Soon these were left behind and the rising space ships approached a cluster which was the main Earth fleet.

Slowly the procession of ships headed inward toward the sun. Pluto grew smaller and smaller as the hours passed until finally it was lost in the blanket of stars that formed an almost uninterrupted screen of light out in space.

Technicians were at work on the robot control bank attached to Gar's brain. One day, when the Earth had begun to loom largely in the firmament ahead, Turlogh and Frances were standing side by side looking out the forward view port. Suddenly they were startled by a familiar voice behind them. They turned in surprise. There stood Gar!

"Gar," Frances cried rushing into his arms.

There were tears in Gar's eyes as he folded his arms about his sister but there was a smile of happiness on his face as he looked over her head at Turlogh. Finally Frances stood back and looked up to her brother.

"Do you feel all right?" she asked.

"Fit as a fiddle," he said.

Frances turned to Turlogh. "Well, come on. Say something," she said to him. "Don't just stand there like an idiot."

"Hello sucker," Turlogh said with a grin. "I hope you will enjoy staying out in space because you can't ever go to Earth."

"Why not," Frances asked in surprise.

"He wouldn't dare to," Turlogh said. It was Gar's turn to look puzzled.

"What do you mean?" he asked.

"Well," Turlogh said with a grin, "here you are and your brain is in the storeroom. You know what they do on Earth to guys that are out of their head, don't you?"

It was several months later back on Earth that Gar, Turlogh, and Frances sat side by side in the rear of a taxi speeding along Michigan Boulevard in Chicago.

"Just like old times, eh?" Turlogh said. Then he added, "Only nicer, now that I know you've got a sister. To think that all these years we've bummed all over the system together you never once mentioned that you had a sister!"

"Well," Gar replied, "you never asked me. Anyway I felt it my duty to protect her from you."

"What does the government say about your brain?" Frances asked.

"There're fixing it up in a sort of a portable motor car," Gar answered. "I don't need it with me because the contact is good over almost any distance, but one of these days soon we will be going back up into space and naturally I'll have to take my brain along."

"Did you say 'we'?" Frances asked.

"Of course he said 'we'," Turlogh broke in. "You don't think we would leave Gar behind do you?"

THE TAXI sped on through the night, with its three passengers silent, each intent on his own thoughts; Frances' anticipating the evening's entertainment before them, and Gar's and Turlogh's by coincidence dwelling on the same things.

Out in space, so far away that the sun became only a dim star competing with others that were light years away, a fleet of ships circled Pluto endlessly. On them were robots which Gar could control through his now repaired control bank. There were weapons and instruments on these ships which would yield secrets that the Earth could use to advantage.

The two men were not thinking of these, however. They were thinking of what these ships could mean to them. A fleet of their own! Atom powered and powerful.

Adventure! With these ships they could travel the spaceways to their hearts' desire. With Gar's mind operating through robots, he could explore the sun, Jupiter, Neptune, and places where living flesh would die instantly.

Gar's thoughts turned to the Mind of Pluto. He missed it here on Earth. After the destruction of Bubble City, Gar had made his first contact with the giant intellect housed in the forest of fantastic growth in the third bubble. Before long he had merged with it and become One with it, almost forgetting his own individuality, and he had learned much and experienced thoughts and feelings beyond the comprehension of ordinary mortals.

Godlike thoughts that could only come from a mind that had lived for millions of centuries as an active, forever young mentality.

As the taxi sped smoothly along, his mind reached out across the vast abyss of space that separated the two worlds and touched briefly that vast Mind, and felt its wisdom and strength flow into him.

The contact comforted him. No matter where he roamed he could always reach out to it and enlist its aid. He could always reach across the void and join it—become One with it.

The mind is a peculiar thing. It is a Unity and yet an infinity. It can set up local centers of awareness that act as separate entities; and these can function as One or as many.

In the normal man the vision centers, the auditory centers, the reasoning centers, and all others, act independently and without interfering with one another. Yet their activity can be joined in higher and ever higher centers so that they become the parts of one mind and person.

With telepathy that is as sure and swift as thought itself, individuals can merge their individual consciousnesses into greater and higher units, so that the many become one vast

Mind that is the functioning of the Whole, as it is with the Forest Mind of Pluto.

The taxi sped on, and only the click of the meter and the little clucking sounds of the tires on the pavement disturbed the silence.

THE END

If you've enjoyed this book, you will not want to miss these terrific titles…

ARMCHAIR SCI-FI & HORROR DOUBLE NOVELS, $12.95 each

D-121 **THE GENIUS BEASTS** by Frederik Pohl
THIS WORLD IS TABOO by Murray Leinster

D-122 **THE COSMIC LOOTERS** by Edmond Hamilton
WANDL THE INVADER by Ray Cummings

D-123 **ROBOT MEN OF BUBBLE CITY** by Rog Phillips
DRAGON ARMY by William Morrison

D-124 **LAND BEYOND THE LENS** by S. J. Byrne
DIPLOMAT-AT-ARMS by Keith Laumer

D-125 **VOYAGE OF THE ASTEROID, THE** by Laurence Manning
REVOLT OF THE OUTWORLDS by Milton Lesser

D-126 **OUTLAW IN THE SKY** by Chester S. Geier
LEGACY FROM MARS by Raymond Z. Gallun

D-127 **THE GREAT FLYING SAUCER INVASION** by Geoff St. Reynard
THE BIG TIME by Fritz Leiber

D-128 **MIRAGE FOR PLANET X** by Stanley Mullen
POLICE YOUR PLANET by Lester del Rey

D-129 **THE BRAIN SINNERS** by Alan E. Nourse
DEATH FROM THE SKIES by A. Hyatt Verrill

D-139 **CRY CHAOS** by Dwight V. Swain
THE DOOR THROUGH SPACE By Marion Zimmer Bradley

ARMCHAIR SCIENCE FICTION CLASSICS, $12.95 each

C-55 **UNDER THE TRIPLE SUNS**
by Stanton A. Coblentz

C-56 **STONE FROM THE GREEN STAR**
by Jack Williamson

C-57 **ALIEN MINDS**
by E. Everett Evans

ARMCHAIR MASTERS OF SCIENCE FICTION SERIES, $16.95 each

G-13 **SCIENCE FICTION GEMS, Vol. Seven**
Jack Vance and others

G-14 **HORROR GEMS, Vol. Seven**
Robert Bloch and others

EXILED ON A LONELY PLANET WITH THE DEVIL

Bulkley was a murdering rat, pure and simple. He had managed to pass the blame for his crimes off onto Frank Newell, who was then convicted and sent into exile on a distant planet. Unfortunately for Newell, Bulkley—in spite of his best, unscrupulous efforts—had also been convicted and sent into exile along with him. So there they were, wanting desperately to spill each other's blood, stranded on a lonely planet together for the rest of their days.

But Newell had discovered something amazing on this heavily vegetated planet— a way to create "men" out of plants. It was a discovery that might help lift his sentence of exile. Unfortunately, Newell's secret fell into the hands of his dread nemesis, Bulkley, who soon had an incredible army of plant-creatures to do his insidious bidding…

CAST OF CHARACTERS

FRANK NEWELL
It seemed so hopeless—he had been exiled on a distant planet with a murderous cad—but then he discovered something…

INDRA HILTON
The odd hat and glasses made her look a bit goofy, but underneath was a beautiful schoolteacher with a penchant for martial arts!

BULKLEY
He wasn't afraid to kill you if it served his purposes. In other words, he was a vicious, murdering thug—but a <u>smart</u> thug.

OLD MAN HILTON aka DR. HYPNO
He was elderly, absent-minded, and liked to babble on forever. Pretty spry for someone on the high side of 121 .

THE CAPTAIN
He had come from space on a rescue mission and wanted to help Newell. The question was whether or not he could trust him.

TOUGH EGG
He was loyal, unswerving, and willing to follow any orders given to him—amazing that he was actually just an overdeveloped tree!

DRAGON ARMY

By
WILLIAM MORRISON

ARMCHAIR FICTION
PO Box 4369, Medford, Oregon 97504

*For more information about Armchair Books and products, visit our
website at...*

www.armchairfiction.com

Or email us at...

armchairfiction@yahoo.com

CHAPTER ONE

FRANK NEWELL was still excited when he heard the beeping of the radio signal at his belt. He put aside the seeds on which he had been working and threw the switch that brought him Bulkley's voice. The man sounded anxious, amusingly so. You might have thought there was real danger. "Newell! You all right?"

Newell tried to keep the excitement out of his own voice. No use betraying his discovery too soon. No sense in giving Bulkley time to start his crafty mind going, to make plans for a double-cross. He said, "I'm fine. How are you? How are all the relatives?"

"Don't try to be funny, Newell." That crack about the relatives must have hurt, to judge from the savage anger in the man's tones. It emphasized his isolation, his desperate loneliness. "A minute ago I was feeling sorry for you. Don't make me want to break your neck myself."

"No, that would be dangerous, wouldn't it?"

"That last fall of trees didn't come close to you?"

"I wasn't among the trees. I was in a cleared area."

"You've got more sense than I thought." He could detect the relief in the man's voice. "For a while I thought you might have been caught. I thought I might be—"

"Can't lose me, Bulkley. It's sweet of you to worry, though. How'd you spare the time from watching that dancer on television?"

"Being funny again, Newell? You know that I don't watch television during the day."

"Thought you just sat there and stared at the screen, mooning about her."

"Newell, if you weren't so important to me—"

"Sure. I know how much you think of me. Anyway, my dear friend, I'm alive. Alive and kicking. I'll be back in two hours."

And with something to tell you, he added to himself. Something that'll give you the kind of hope you haven't had in a long time. We're no pals, we hate each other's guts, but all the same we're in this for another three months, at least—if we live that long.

It's a big *if,* he thought, as he turned back to the seeds. This beautiful planet, so quiet and peaceful now, is a death trap. It's a planet where danger lies in wait. That's why Bulkley and I have been exiled here.

He thought back. *How long have we been there together? Why, it's no more than six months in all. Imagine that, only six months! It feels like a lifetime. But six months with Bulkley would be a lifetime anywhere.*

The man never fooled me, he reflected with gloomy pride. *I hated him from the beginning, although not the way I've come to hate him now. That's because I've come to realize what he's done to me. That night when the truth struck me—that's the time I needed self-control. That was the time when the desire to avenge myself, to kill, surged over me, almost overpowered me. But it would have left me alone here, alone on this damned and beautiful planet.*

So I kept my feelings under control and, after a time, they changed. My hatred for Bulkley is deeper now. But it's become a cold, calculating hatred. Some day I'm going to have my revenge. But not yet. Now we have to work together, protect each other as if there were the greatest bond of affection between us. We need each other too much for either of us to let the other die.

BROTHERLY love, he thought. Brotherly love, just like Cain and Abel in the prehistoric story.

Newell began to sort his seeds again. He was a big man in shorts, a thin film of moisture covering his deeply bronzed skin. The pinkish sun was hot overhead, and there was no wind at all. Only the creeping plants in the forest crackled from time to time in response to some inner change in their metabolism.

When he had finished with his seeds, his hands almost dropping some of them in his excitement, it was late, more than time to return to the plastex hut. He put everything in order for the next day's experiments, and set out for home.

The forest was still quiet, but once a slight wind arose, and he had a sensation of danger, and an urge to run. Don't be a fool, he told himself. There's no danger, nothing to run from. He fought down the sense of panic, and forced himself to walk slowly.

Outside the plastex hut he forced himself to stop. No use letting Bulkley see how fundamentally excited he was. For a long time they had been without hope of escape, and now that one unexpected door away from death had been opened, Bulkley would be in a fever of anticipation. No use letting the man see the eagerness, the hope that filled Newell himself at the thought of what he had discovered.

As he had expected, Bulkley was sitting at the television set, his eyes glued to the screen. A lithe girl, clothed mostly in veils of gauze, twisted and writhed against an exotic purple and gold background. The same girl. This was the kind of educational program Bulkley liked, he told himself with a grim smile. It was a program that specialized in graphic illustration of the anthropology of alien planets, with occasional excursions into the anthropology of the dead past. It combined sex with instruction. A fine program, a fascinating program, a program well calculated to drive a lonely man completely crazy.

Almost incidentally, Newell noted the dancer's face. It was half hidden by the swirling gauze; but he could see that it was wistful and appealing. Bulkley had probably not even noticed it, nor had he noted the name of the program chastely displayed on a glowing placard at the right: EXTINCT DANCES OF EARTH. Bulkley was too busy watching those lithe movements, anticipating the throwing off of the next veil.

With a feeling of unexpected pleasure, Newell allowed himself to show a small part of the hatred he felt. As the dancing girl whirled with flaring veils, he reached over and turned off the set. The girl faded out.

Silence descended on the hut. The rows of transparent metal utensils hanging on the wall, the clothes, transparent and opaque, neatly arrayed in the closets, the store of precious raw plastex powder in the stock roam, the tiny atomic power plant at the side—all were silent. Silent and tense, as if waiting for a thunderbolt to strike from the equally silent sky.

The thunderclouds were forming. A blank look spread over Bulkley's face. Then, as he realized to the full the deliberateness of the act, he leaped to his feet, his hand dropping to his holster. "I'll get you for that, you lousy space-warped fool!"

THE MAN'S rage was destined to be frustrated, and that made it amusing. Newell smiled, and dropped into a seat. "Calm down," he said. "I've got something important to say to you. And you'd be in no condition to appreciate it after watching that program."

"I'll watch what I damn please, you mind-twisted—"

"Easy, Bulkley, or you'll run out of adjectives. And I get tired of hearing you repeat yourself. You know that you don't watch what you please. You watch what the censors let you. And they'd never permit the girl to strip off the last veil."

Bulkley was still cursing, more to himself now than at the other man. Newell stared at him, his own excitement more easily controlled now that he saw what a fool his companion looked like when he was unreasonably excited. And yet, Bulkley was no fool. He was a shrewd, dangerous enemy, and a false and treacherous friend. Physically, he was enormously impressive. Tall, wide-shouldered, with powerful muscles that had been hardened in his work as engineer on numerous planets, he seemed to dwarf even Newell. He was older than Newell, and—yes, Newell had to admit it—shrewder. Bulkley had been around; he knew how things were done. Newell was a good biochem man, with a special affinity for plants. He could almost sense how a plant felt as it grew—and that seemed absurd, because a plant has no feelings. But Bulkley could sense how *people* felt.

He had control, too, a control and a will as strong, when he wanted to use them, as Newell's own. His hot rage was disappearing now, and as it disappeared, a cold and ugly look formed in his eyes. A cold look in the eyes, a cold smile on the hard face. He said evenly, "One of these days, Newell, I'm going to kill you for pulling a little trick like that."

"Kill me? You should thank me, Bulkley. All you're building up for yourself by watching programs of that sort is frustration. You haven't a chance in the world—any world—of seeing a girl like her in the flesh for a long time. Why tantalize yourself? It only makes your blood pressure worse. And there are no doctors on this planet to treat it."

"You're so kind and thoughtful of my health, Newell. I don't know how to thank you. But I'm going to kill you anyway. I'm warning you now."

"You won't kill me yet, though. We're the only two people on this planet. You need me too much."

"One of these days you might make me forget that I need you."

NEWELL stood up slowly. "I won't tell you my opinion of you, Bulkley," he said. "I'll leave it to you to guess. But I don't want you to think I'm afraid of you. If there were such a thing as a space-devil, I wouldn't be afraid of that either, not if I hated it as much as I hate you. And another thing I don't want you to imagine is that you've fooled me. Because you haven't, not worth a damn. I know why I'm on this planet. It's because you framed me and had me put here."

"You're having hallucinations, Newell."

"I don't think so. I've been having thoughts. We've been here for about six months now—and I've had time to figure out why I was convicted."

"The why is simple enough. You were caught." There was a contemptuous sneer on the bigger man's face. "They had the evidence against you, just as they had against me. Only the big shot who arranged everything got away."

"The big shot? There was no big shot. It was you who ran everything, you who manufactured the evidence. It's no use trying to laugh that off, Bulkley, because I know the truth. Millions of credits were disappearing, and you were the one responsible for making them disappear. When they got wise to you, you tried to shift the blame to me. That didn't work—not quite, anyway. You couldn't get out of the net of evidence yourself, although you were able to involve me."

"And you were innocent. Too bad."

"I was a simple-minded scientist. Before this happened I had been entirely absorbed in my work. When the accusations against me were first made, I was too bewildered to know what was happening. It probably wouldn't have made any difference if I had known. The evidence I needed had disappeared. The entire Research Bureau where I worked had been cleaned out. The only way I might have been cleared was by the testimony of the people who were your own pals—the secretary of the Bureau, his assistant, and the others."

"Imagination, Newell. These people were no pals of mine. Especially after they disappeared, and couldn't be located again."

"Could the reason for that be, my friend, that you dipped your hands in a little murder?"

Bulkley's face flushed suddenly at the question as a wave of blood swept up from the neckline. Put he didn't lose his temper again. He was icy now, icy and more dangerous.

"It could be…" he said slowly, "…if that's the kind of imagination you have."

"It is." Newell laughed harshly. "You have no idea. Bulkley, how close you were to death the night you confessed."

"I confessed?"

"You were talking and cursing in your sleep. I guess that the loneliness here was getting you. I heard you through the walls. I opened the door of your room and listened."

"And you didn't say anything in the morning?"

"I didn't trust myself to speak to you. That was the morning I got up early and hurried to work before you awoke."

Bulkley said slowly, "I remember that you did act strange for a time. I thought that the loneliness was getting you."

"Not loneliness. The urge to murder. Yes, Bulkley, it's catching. I think the chief reason I didn't kill you—"

"The same reason I let you live. We need each other too much."

NEWELL nodded. "To keep our sanity, if for no other reason. They put us together on this planet, out of the way of the great galactic routes, with no hope of returning to civilization. I don't know whether they figured we hated each other or not. At any rate, it was a clever method of punishment to leave us here together."

He stared through the clear plastex window. "As pretty a little planet as you'd want to see. Food for the taking, and clear sweet water in every brook. Not an animal in the place, so they didn't leave us weapons. But they were kind to us, so far as kindness can be consistent with the cruelty of punishment. They left us books, a television receiver, a supply of raw material for plastex, and a stock of drugs in case of dangerous virus or bacterial disease. They wanted us to stay alive as long as possible—until one of those little accidents happened."

He was silent for a moment, as both he and Bulkley thought of the accident they had recently so narrowly escaped. Long streamers from the pink sun, a violent windstorm, the giant trees snapping and striking out in all directions—death had been very close that night. It would be close again the next time the winds rose, and it would never cease threatening from the earthquakes, the damnable earthquakes that had eventually destroyed every colony that had been started here. Sooner or later, the earthquakes would engulf them.

Not yet, however. And possibly, not at all, if his new hopes were justified.

Bulkley said, "Is this what you wanted to tell me?"

"No. This is merely something I want to get off my chest, so that we can have things straight, and understand each other. The fact is that I've stumbled on something that may be important enough to get us off this planet."

He could see the spark of light that sprang into Bulkley's eyes. There was new hope there—new hope, and new danger.

"What is it, Newell?"

"Before I tell you, I want to know how far you've gone with that equipment you've been working on, from the old buried wreck we found in the forest."

The man's eyes became hooded, evasive. "Not very far. The spaceship was an obsolete type, and the equipment wasn't of much use."

"Then there's no use in my telling you what I found."

"What do you mean by that?" demanded Bulkley.

"We can't get off here unless we can communicate with the nearest space outpost. And if you haven't been able to construct a long-range radio transmitter..."

THE EYES shifted, prepared to look candid and truthful. "I haven't been working on it very hard. I might get the thing done if there was a good reason for it."

You're lying, thought Newell. Most probably you've got the radio transmitter already made, and you're trying to keep its existence to yourself. Now that you see a chance of getting out of here, you feel that your need for me is less. I know you're a killer. I know that I'm dangerous to you, too dangerous to be allowed to live. Well, I'm not going to tell you much now, old friend. I'm not going to tell you so much that you'll feel you can afford to kill me, and go it alone.

He said, "There's a good reason. But I'm keeping it to myself until I see that transmitter."

Bulkley stared at him, hatred radiating from the big body. "So after coming in here and turning that show off, and building up my hopes, you've got nothing to tell me."

"Nothing, until I see that transmitter. I don't trust you, Bulkley. It's never good policy to trust murderers."

The hatred in the room seemed ready to crystallize, to take tangible form. But Bulkley merely said with contempt, "You'll see the transmitter tomorrow. And what you have to say had better be good."

"It will be good enough." Newell switched on the television set. An ancient man's withered face sprang into being on the screen, and a droning voice began to fill the air with details of linguistic differences between races of different galaxies. This was educational, and no mistake about it. "Here's your program, Bulkley. Only, this old bird isn't removing any veils."

Bulkley reached a heavy hand toward the set, and once more the picture on the screen faded. The hatred in the room continued to hang there, thick and heavy.

They ate in silence, and when the meal was over, Newell went into his own room, closed the door, and quietly arranged the booby trap he had prepared. He knew that

Bulkley would not try to kill him yet, not until he had learned what the discovery was. But there was nothing to prevent Bulkley from knocking him out, tying him up, and then torturing him in an effort to get the secret. Nothing but his own ingenuity.

He slept well, too well. In the middle of the night he was awakened by the hoarse scream of a man in terror.

THE BOOBY trap had worked. He flashed on the light. On the floor were a gun and a length of rope. Standing in the doorway was Bulkley, writhing desperately in the grip of long brown arms that hugged his neck with deadly affection, tightened around his body, twisted around his legs. The arms were attached to no body of their own. They hung loose in the air, like the snakes which on this planet did not exist.

It was not good to see a man so terrified, even a man like Bulkley, whose intentions were so obviously murderous. Newell felt a little sick at the sight.

The arms around the neck twisted tighter, and the screams became hoarser and more strangled. Newell realized that in another minute the man would lose consciousness.

He pressed the button of one of his research flashlights. A strong invisible pencil of infrared lanced out at the brown arms. They froze into immobility.

He said quietly, "They won't get any tighter, Bulkley. Not unless you start them up again by trying to escape."

The other man was deadly still. Not a muscle seemed to move, although he could not keep an artery in his neck from twitching, and his sweat glands were over-stimulated by fear. His face glistened in the dim light like the surface of a sheet of water.

Newell said with contempt, "I thought you'd try to do that. You probably caught the others asleep too. It's too bad for you that my own ropes were a little more alert than yours."

Terror found a voice. Bulkley said hoarsely, "Let me out of these damned things."

"No, my friend. I don't trust you out of them. They're one of the native plants I've been working with for the past few months. Ordinarily they're harmless, but I've learned how to control them, and to defend myself with them. And I'm defending myself now."

Bulkley stammered, "Let me out. I can't breathe."

"That's hardly something for me to worry about. However, I will loosen them a bit. But I don't intend to remove them, Bulkley. From now on, they stay on you, day and night, until you're no longer in a position to harm me. You may be glad to know that they respond to sudden motions, and if you try any more of your tricks, they'll strangle you for good."

"I won't try anything. Just let me out!"

Newell altered the wavelength emitted in the light pencil, and gave the brown arms a carefully regulated dose of the differently colored infrared. The arms seemed to relax slightly and he heard the long gasping intake of breath from the other man.

"That should let you move around more freely. Now, I think, we'd better get some more sleep."

The man staggered out toward his own room. Newell lay down on his bed again, and this time he slept till morning.

CHAPTER TWO

THE PLANET had an approximately twenty-five-hour day, and the nights during the present season were long. When he finally arose, Newell felt rested and pleased with himself. He could hardly say as much for his fellow exile, who was still wearing his animate chains.

Newell ate a hearty meal but, naturally enough, Bulkley had no appetite. His throat was sore from the experience of the night, and his voice was hoarse as he pleaded, "Take these things off me, Newell, and I swear I won't try to kill you again."

Newell laughed without amusement. "Let's not talk nonsense," he said contemptuously. "They're my guarantee against murder." He added, with an air of assurance that Bulkley could not know was false. "Kill me, and you'll never get out. You'll rot with those things around your neck. Now, I'd like to see that radio transmitter,"

As he had expected, it was in the ruins of the old spaceship. Even handicapped as Bulkley was by the brown plant arms around his neck, it took the man only a few minutes to fit the parts together.

Newell stared at the array of tubes and transistors, at the plute-powered electric generator. "Power plant too weak for twenty-four-hour operation, but strong enough to get through to the nearest space station in bursts. Very good. You're not a bad engineer, Bulkley. A little untrustworthy, with homicidal tendencies, but highly skilled."

The man said nothing. But Bulkley clearly had thoughts running through his mind, and the nature of his thoughts was obvious.

Newell hesitated. It seemed foolish to go ahead with keeping a promise to a man who had tried to kill him, but Newell had always kept his word before, and he did not intend to break it now. "All right, Bulkley," he said at last. "Now I'm going to keep my part of the bargain. Come with me."

Newell led the way to the prairie-like field where he had been working. From the corner of his eye he kept a watch on the other man, as if he didn't quite count on the deadly plants to keep Bulkley up to the proper behavior. He knew, as he didn't want Bulkley to know, that the plants had only a short life, and that in the normal course of events it would be only a day or two more before the man was free of them.

The field was bare and looked recently plowed. The normal plant life had been killed off, and the half-acre of brownish-black soil had a stark and naked appearance.

Newell stretched out a hand filled with curious objects. "Take a look at these. What do you think they are?"

Bulkley caught his breath in surprise. "Teeth! Big, pointed brown and white teeth. There are animals on this planet after all!"

He stared around him in an obvious access of terror. The planet had been bad enough before, with its great falls of trees and its earthquakes. Now it seemed to be acquiring new and equally horrible dangers.

But Newell said reassuringly, "There are no animals. Now, get back and watch."

Newell had a plastic bag full of the brown tooth-like objects, and he slung the bag over his shoulder before he walked through the plowed area. As he strode between the furrows, scattering the seed sparsely to right and left, and reaching into the plastic bag from time to time for another handful, he looked like one of the ancient prehistoric farmers back on the mother planet.

FEAR GAVE way to confusion in Bulkley's baffled face. "What do you expect to grow?"

Newell didn't answer. He glanced once at the rapidly rising sun, pink and hot, and then moved on rapidly. He was completing the sowing of the last furrow before he turned to look back.

On the other side of the field, tiny shoots of purple and green were already showing. They pushed up slowly, imperceptibly at times, and then again in sudden spurts, like the minute hands of an ancient timepiece whose mechanism worked jerkily. When the first shoots had reached a height of six inches, the last shoots on the other side of the field were just beginning to break through.

"They're growing fast," said Bulkley, his personal woes momentarily forgotten at the amazing sight.

Newell had rejoined him. "I've learned how to accelerate growth."

"Where'd you get the chemicals you needed?"

"From the other plants. I made extracts. A chemist would have a field day with the variety of different compounds these plants contain. Alkaloids of entirely new types, indole-aliphatic acids, everything. I've been able to extract fairly pure mixtures that will stimulate the kind of growth I want, help twist the plant in the direction I want it to take."

"Then those brown and white things were not teeth, but seeds."

"Yes. Their natural color is white. The treatment I gave them turned them partly brown. But watch."

Some of the plants were almost two feet in height. So far they had grown straight up, apparently without putting forth shoots or branches of any kind. Now there began to grow what seemed like the beginnings of branches. On the top, a small brown swelling began to form.

Slowly the branches developed, one on each side, slowly the brown swellings grew. As the men watched, the shoots divided at the bottom. The growing plants began to look like caricatures of human beings, fantastic scarecrows that arose from the incredibly nourishing soil.

When they had reached four feet in height, the plants were more human than ever, uncannily so. The purple had disappeared, and now they looked like brown men, their faces and bodies streaked with white. Bulkley was silent, his eyes filled with wonder and a new fear. There was something else, too. Newell thought he could detect the beginnings of crafty calculations.

Still the plants continued to grow, both in height and in width. And as they grew, they became more human.

Newell gazed with awe at the thing that he himself had wrought. Science it was, the mere application of simple and easily understood principles—the use of plant hormones, light, heat, and other simple agents, which he had not troubled to explain to Bulkley—and yet the results struck him as a miracle.

The crop he had sown filled the expanse of field before him. Brown and white manlike things writhed and grimaced as the stimulating rays of the hot sun reached them. Rows and rows of them, at least two thousand in number, an aura of power, of energy barely held in leash, surrounded them. They began to twist from side to side, as if in anger at the roots that still held them to the ground, as if trying to escape and wreak vengeance on some enemy yet unknown.

Newell was reminded of the ancient legend of Cadmus, who had planted dragon's teeth and seen the teeth grow into an army of soldiers, whom a trivial incident had provoked into deadly combat. But nothing would set these soldiers off, he thought. His control of them was too good.

The pencil of Newell's flash beam widened into a conical ray, swept over the field. Where it struck, one brown manlike thing after another froze into a posture of tortured strength of motion held temporarily in check by a force that could not last. The field seemed to overflow with a great uneasy quiet.

And then the quiet was shattered, the sun in the sky blazed like a nova and blotted out the strange sight. Newell dropped to the ground, while behind him there came from Bulkley a harsh laugh of triumph.

WHEN HE awoke, it was dark. He was lying on his own bed, unbound. He had no idea of how much time had passed, of how long he had lain unconscious. But his head throbbed painfully, and through it there passed a series of harsh noises, of shrieks and cries that grated on his nerves. As he lifted himself to a sitting position, the noises began to make sense. He realized that they were the sounds from a television program to which Bulkley was listening.

They were weird, shrill, piercing. Exotic music, he told himself. Music to accompany a dance such as that he had turned off—how long before? The program was repeated every two days. That meant that he had lain unconscious for at least a day and a half.

He wondered what Bulkley had learned in that time. More than was safe he was sure of. Enough, he feared, to do tremendous harm.

Newell forced himself to his feet and staggered to the door. As he pulled it open, a pair of brown and white hands gripped him, one from each side. Bulkley, at the television set, grunted. "Time you woke up."

Through still dazed eyes, Newell stared at the creatures holding him, the creatures that he himself had changed from plants into the semblances of men.

Bulkley said quietly, "You made a bad mistake, Newell. Those ropes you had on me were slackening just enough to let me get at them. First I slashed the ones around my neck with a knife, and then I was able to get at the others—and at you."

"And now you control these creatures." It was not a question, but a flat statement of fact—of sickening fact.

"Thanks to a couple of notebooks of yours. You gave me credit before for being a good engineer, Newell. I give you credit now for being a good biologist. You worked out the details so well that it was a cinch to follow them. And when I found your notebooks in your room, I knew that I'd be able to do with these creatures as I pleased."

As he talked, his eyes remained fastened to the screen. The same dancer whom Newell had turned off on the previous occasion was now performing again, this time almost fully clothed. Now he could catch quick glimpses of her face as she whirled rapidly around, see what genuine charm she possessed. Now he could wonder if Bulkley was quite so irrational in wanting her, in dreaming about her.

Bulkley said, "These things were easy to condition. At first I used lights of different wavelengths, then spoken commands along with the lights. I just followed your notes all along. The things learned faster than dogs or monkeys. It was no trouble at all to get them to respond to spoken commands alone. All I had to do was talk loud, so that they would be sure to catch the sound in their vibration-detecting organs. It's almost as if they had brains."

Newell said dully, "They have, in a way. They have central motor control in the upper part of the chest—or in what would be the upper part of the chest in a man."

"That explains it. But certain kinds of things they don't learn. I've tried them with heat rays, mechanical shock, chemical poisoning. They react, but they don't learn fear. That means they don't feel. And that's perfect for the things I intend to do with them."

THE CREATURES beside Newell made no sound. They were as motionless as the species of plants from which they had descended. But they gave an impression of alertness, of waiting, that was more human than plantlike.

"Let me show you some of the things I can get them to do," said Bulkley. He put his fingers to his mouth and whistled shrilly.

Two more of the creatures came through the door of the hut. "Take fire," said Bulkley.

One of them picked up a fuel lighter with one stubby hand and set the flame to the end of his other arm. The material charred, flickered, and then caught fire. The expression on what passed for a face did not change.

"Put out," ordered Bulkley.

The flaming arm thrust against the side of the hut and put out the fire. Again the expression on what so horribly resembled a human face remained unaltered.

"That'll give you an idea. They'll do anything they're conditioned to do—and I know how to condition them. I haven't given them very complicated commands as yet, but they're learning fast. And there are two thousand of them."

"They're dangerous, Bulkley." Newell's head was clearing, and he was beginning to realize what the other man intended. "They may burn their arms as ordered, but you're really the one who's playing with fire."

"I'll take my chances of their turning on me. I've got them under control. And I've got you there too."

The dance came to an end, and he switched off the set. "I've got a little business to attend to, Newell. A million or so miles off this planet." He noticed Newell's surprise, and grinned evilly. "I can't get as far, yet, as the next planet. But that wrecked ship had better parts than I let you know. It even had several lifeboats, almost intact. I've taken parts of those boats and built myself a low-powered one-man jet job that'll help me get more supplies. If a few hours from now you shift that screen from the entertainment channels to some of the automatic space scanners, you'll be able to see what I do. I think that what happens will keep you entertained. But don't try to get away."

The door closed behind Bulkley and two of the creatures. The other two, their hand-like appendages on Newell's own arms, relaxed their grip, but remained at his side.

Newell took a deep breath, and tried to think. He knew better than to believe he was free. A dog could be trained in a few weeks, *was* trained in the old days, to be an effective canine soldier, to watch with a fierce vigilance every move you made, to tear you apart if you tried to pull a gun or other object recognizable as a weapon. These plant-creatures learned faster than dogs, and were more dangerous. He himself, during his first experiments, had been thrilled to see how rapidly they could be conditioned, with what incredible speed they could go through the motions of learning.

Of their physical strength he had only a rough idea. Flexible plant fibers could be as tough as animal muscles, but that was not where the chief danger lay. What set them apart, what made them horrible beyond the ancient breeds of great cats and feral dogs, and the six-legged harpies of such planets as Venus IV, or any of the other fierce beasts at which primitive humans had once shuddered, was the fact of their insensitivity to feeling. Neither happiness nor pain affected them. They were plant robots who, if once started on their course, let nothing stand in their way. You had to destroy them completely in order to stop them.

No, Bulkley was not being careless, as he himself had been. It made Newell sick to recall exactly how careless he had been. He had forgotten that the plants that held the man captive weakened and relaxed their grip under the direct rays of the sun. In his excitement at seeing the army of growing creatures, he had behaved like a fool.

HE SWITCHED on the set, the two plant-creatures watching without any motion of their own. The light receptors, which were scattered over the entire upper halves of their bodies, were so small as to be invisible to the naked eye. But not the slightest move, he knew, would escape them.

A dim picture appeared on the scene; a voice came soothingly from the speaker. "Do you have difficulty falling asleep? Do you suffer unnecessarily from insomnia? Do your troubles keep you awake? Then tune in our special program with Dr. Hypno! Dr. Hypno's soothing personality will put you to sleep without difficulty over millions of miles of space. Dr. Hypno's healing balm for the soul will act as the salve for your wounded psyche.

"Dr. Hypno is brought to you as a good will service by Psychiatric Associates, Inc., makers of psychic articles of all kinds. In just a moment, Psychiatric Associates, Inc. will bring you the details of a wonderful offer by which you can obtain absolutely free some of the most remarkable inventions…"

He leaned forward to turn the thing off, when suddenly, responding to something in his behavior that must have set off an alarm mechanism, the two creatures seized him and held him firm. He was helpless, unable to move forward or back.

The eyes of Dr. Hypno widened, became enormous, and began to glow. A camera trick, he thought dully. But he could not turn his own eyes away. Nor could he close his ears when a soothing voice began, "You are falling asleep, you are falling—asleep."

He slept.

Strangely enough, he felt refreshed when he awoke. A post-hypnotic suggestion by Dr. Hypno, he thought.

He had his freedom to move once more. Carefully, for fear of alarming the too-alert creatures, he leaned forward and shifted the screen from the entertainment channels to the space scanners.

The space scanners, he knew, were scattered along the main passenger and freighter routes. They were like the ancient buoys on the oceans of water-rich planets, informing sea-faring vessels of their positions. But unlike the buoys, these scanners had automatic television cameras attached. In case a vessel met with some disaster and its own sending set was destroyed, some scanner or other was sure to pick up its position and guide a protest ship to the rescue.

On the screen, a tiny silvery figure swam into view. Slowly it grew larger, became a giant shape that blotted out more and more of the background of stars. It was a freighter, speeding in a trajectory, which at its closest point would bring the ship to within two million miles of his own planet.

From out of the blackness, a tiny gnat appeared and raced after the freighter. From a gleaming point, the gnat grew, took on definite form. It was a low-powered atomic jet ship of the most primitive design, resembling the one-man jets of the pre-spaceflight era. Speed was high, but the jet was so small that the oxygen store, despite the regenerators, could hardly suffice for mare than a few million miles. He could see vaguely the figure of the man inside. That was Bulkley, so intent on pursuit. That was the murderer, going about new murders.

A flash of light appeared at the muzzle of one of the weapons of the jet and, almost simultaneously, the side of the freighter burst open like a great eggshell. In the heatless vacuum of interstellar space there was no sound. But the great flash of radiation was as terrifying as any roar would have been. The entire screen shone with fierce radiance and then blanked out. The sending scanner had been put out of commission.

CHAPTER THREE

HE TURNED off the set altogether, his heart sick, his body tense with excitement. A few hours from now, what remained of the freighter would crash on the surface of the planet. Until then, he had time to think. He had time to find a way out of the horrible mess into which his own blundering had brought him.

He stared once more at the two plant-creatures that were guarding him. *Strange,* he thought, *that they don't look absolutely alike. The arrangement of white streaks on the brown surface is different in each case. They had different individualities. The one on my right looks tough, hard-boiled, but the other one seems to have a kinder expression. They deserve names. Think I'll christen them Tough-Egg and Kind-Mugg.*

Then he laughed at himself. I'm trying to read their expressions as if those were human faces, he told himself. I'm ascribing human emotions to them. They're not human, they're plants. They have no feelings, one way or the other.

No feelings at all. They can be used for any purpose Bulkley wants to use them. Committing more murders, for instance.

I'll have to stop him, somehow, figure out away. They're conditioned to taking orders from him, but I'll have to recondition them. Let me see now...they're affected primarily by chemical changes, and by light. Sounds as such mean little to them. They get the mechanical vibrations, but conditioning to words comes *after* strong conditioning to different lights. If I had my flashlights—

Trouble is, there aren't any flashlights. There are no sources of adjustable light or heat within the room. Bulkley has been thoughtful enough to remove them. Still, Bulkley can't think of everything. Maybe he made a mistake, as I did. Maybe—ah, the television set.

He moved cautiously, slowly, so that the creatures would not be stimulated by any sudden motion to pounce upon him. He switched on the set again, then turned it around, opened the back, and stared inside. No glowing tubes here. But I can feel a slight warmth when I put my hand close. And those plant-things are thermotropic, they respond to heat radiations.

He turned the set so that the faint heat was directed at Tough-Egg. The plant-creature moved forward, hesitated—then moved forward again. Responds to stimulus, thought Newell, but it's a weak stimulus, and a weak response. Can't recondition him—*it*—that way. But it's a start. And maybe Kind-Mugg will respond more strongly.

Kind-Mugg didn't respond at all. Newell muttered to himself in disappointment. Have to try something else he realized. Have to keep on trying. Maybe by the time Bulkley gets back I'll have hit on something good.

'The hours passed in almost futile experiments. By the time he heard the rockets of the torn freighter, decelerating what was left of the ship for a landing, he had learned little. But the two creatures left to guard him had become almost like old friends. No doubt about it, they had distinct individualities. No feelings, though. No more feelings than two pieces of furniture.

THE DOOR opened. Bulkley stepped in and grinned at him. "Still here I see, Newell."

"I saw what you did to that freighter."

"Neat job, wasn't it? I needed supplies I couldn't get off that wrecked ship on this planet. And when I tuned in on shipping news I heard that this freighter would be coming along with some of the objects I needed."

"You won't get away with it for long, Bulkley. You caught them by surprise because they never expected pirates in this part of space. But the patrol guards have the news by now. They'll be sending a well-armed patrol ship along in a day or so. And you'll be helpless against them."

"Not helpless, Newell. I know exactly how I'm going to handle any patrol ship that shows up. In fact I'm looking forward to it. The more ships they send, the more supplies I'll have."

The hatred in the man twisted his face into a horrible smile. Newell felt hatred of his own well up inside him at the thought of what the man intended to do.

Bulkley could see how he felt. "Don't like the idea, do you, Newell? Don't like the idea of all those patrol guards being cut down like the worthless space-lice they are? Too bad. Because you're going to help me. That's why I'm letting you stay alive, Newell. You're going to be very useful to me. And you're going to start off by getting me some more of those dragon-tooth seeds."

Newell's teeth clamped together. He shook his head.

Bulkley smiled grimly. "You'll change your mind, Newell. This is too important for me to let you be stubborn about it. Do you realize what I can do with these creatures?"

"I realize. That's why I won't help you."

Bulkley seemed not to have heard him. "The perfect robots," he said, as if to himself. "Trained to do anything I want them to, anything at all. No feelings, no fears. And they're cheaper than any other kind of robot. No expensive machinery to make, no sponge-colloid brain that can go out of order. The kind for which people like me have been looking for a long time.

"They're not only perfect servants, Newell, they're soldiers. What was the old word for them—cannon fodder? That's what they are. They don't know what it is to live, so they don't mind dying. No indoctrination needed, no nonsense about how terrible the enemy is. Just train them to obey, and they kill for you and get themselves killed."

The man has delusions of grandeur, thought Newell. He wasn't crazy—far from it. In some ways he was only too sane. But hatred consumed him, and on this lonely planet his hatred had been too greatly bottled up. Now it had its chance to come out. And when it came, it would bring death and destruction in its wake.

"So you see, my friend, why I want more of those dragon teeth."

"They're not easy to prepare," said Newell slowly. He was beginning to get the glimmering of an idea that might keep him safe for a while. Bulkley needed him. Why not pretend to go along with what Bulkley wanted, pretend he wouldn't dare disobey—and at the same time put a spoke in the man's plans? "They grow fast once you put them in the ground," he went on, "but before that, they need a good deal of treatment. That takes time."

"Then get started. These two creatures will watch you and serve as your assistants. Maybe, if the process isn't too complicated, they'll learn how to prepare the seeds themselves. That would be nice, wouldn't it, Newell? The cannon fodder themselves preparing more cannon fodder." He laughed, and suddenly, without warning, changed the subject. "By the way, Newell, we have guests on our beautiful planet. Not the, kind of guests I'd have chosen, but they'll do to relieve the loneliness."

The crew, thought Newell—some of the crew were still alive.

Bulkley flashed a light signal through the window. The door opened, and a man and a woman, guarded by two of the plant-creatures, stumbled over the threshold.

"Mr. Hilton," said Bulkley. The man peered at them from behind thin transparent metal lenses, the high retractive index making his eyes seem enormous. His face was old, lined, worried. He was a hundred and twenty if a day, thought Newell. "And this is Miss Indra Hilton, his daughter."

The girl stared at him dully through her own glasses, the shock of what had happened during the past few hours still visible on her face. An atomic blast that tore out the side of the freighter was not an easy thing to take, thought Newell. Still, those glasses, and those clothes... She'd have been pretty, he told himself, in the right clothes. But perhaps it was just as well, for her sake, that she wasn't pretty. She wore an octagonal hat, as well as octagonal glasses—as weird a combination as a girl could be expected to think up. She looked school-teacherish in the worst sense of the word. Her clothes were awkward, loose-fitting, the kind some women seemed to choose almost automatically in an effort to conceal any good points they might have. But she wasn't old. No clothes could make so young a girl seem old. She wasn't past her early twenties.

"This, my honored guests," said Bulkley, "is my very talented colleague, Mr. Newell. Mr. Newell invented those plant creatures that are now guarding you. But he doesn't like what I'm doing with them, so that he is a prisoner just as much as you are."

Newell found his voice. "What happened to the crew?"

"The members of the crew were unfortunately killed in the...the *accident,* shall we call it? That incapacitated the freighter. Mr. Hilton brought the ship down here with the mechanical landing equipment, setting the controls according to instructions I radioed to him. Mr. Hilton is very good at following instructions."

"I am an educator," said Hilton sonorously. "Yes, gentlemen, I instruct the young in the best knowledge of the past. It is a noble profession, and it trains the mind in proper habits of thought." His voice didn't sound old. It was strong and resonant, and Newell thought it seemed faintly familiar. He wondered whether at any time in the past the man had taught at a school that he had attended. Greater Procyon IV University, for instance, where he had taken special courses in chemo-botany, had thousands of teachers, and most of them he knew only by sight, if at all.

"Miss Hilton also teaches school," said Bulkley. He grinned again. "It seems to me that she could stand learning a few things herself. I'll be glad to teach them to her."

THERE WAS a tense silence in the room. In Newell the feeling of hatred suddenly welled up almost to the point of bursting. He felt a choking sensation in his throat, and in his muscles an almost intolerable urge to leap forward and smash Bulkley's evilly grinning face. Perhaps, though, that was exactly what the man wanted. Perhaps that was what he counted on, knowing that if any move were made against him, his planet robots would immediately spring to his defense.

Only the old man seemed undisturbed by the threat. He took off his metal lenses and began to polish them. "It is always good to add to one's knowledge," he announced sonorously. The old boy is senile thought Newell. He doesn't understand a thing. But the look of dignity on the old face gave him pause. "Maybe he's just a little slow on the uptake," thought Newell. "Or maybe he's putting on an act."

The old man held up the lenses, stared through them. "Now his face, as well as his voice, seems familiar," thought Newell. "Where in space have I seen him?"

Bulkley waited, as if disappointed that no outburst had occurred. He grunted. "I think that Miss Hilton is disappointed in me. I've really neglected her. Perhaps she doesn't realize the effect that traveling in almost gravity-less space has on a man. It leaves one unable to think for a time of the more pleasant things in life. But you needn't worry about me, Miss Hilton. I'm very glad you're here, even if you don't exactly resemble some of the performers on interspatial television."

'Something clicked in Newell's mind. He knew now where he had seen the old man before.

Bulkley said, "I'm going to see what I can do with some of those supplies on the freighter. Meanwhile, Newell, make our guests at home. And don't try to escape—any of you. These plant creatures are too alert. And they can't be bought, bribed, or won over in any manner whatever."

He went out, leaving them together. Newell said politely, "I've seen you before, Mr. Hilton. On television. You're no schoolteacher. You're Dr. Hypno."

"Yes, my dear sir. I am Dr. Hypno."

"I had trouble recognizing you. Even now your face doesn't look quite the same—but the special cameras will account for that."

The man nodded. "I am, however, actually an educator, a schoolteacher, as you so crudely put it. I had dabbled for many years in hypnosis as a cultural activity, and when this firm, Psychiatric Associates, Inc., needed some one of ability, I was recommended to them."

"Can you hypnotize Bulkley?"

"Not, I fear under present conditions, against his will. Not without special equipment."

"Perhaps that can be obtained." He turned to face the girl. "Any special talents of your own, Miss Hilton, that we could use against Bulkley?"

For some unaccountable reason, the girl flushed. "I am a schoolteacher too," she said. "My father and I had decided to splurge on a vacation together. Freighter rates are lower than regular passenger rates, of course, because freighters lack certain conveniences. That is why we were so unfortunate as to fall into your partner's hands."

"Don't call Bulkley my partner." The girl's eyebrows went up in a manner that was strangely out of place for a schoolteacher. "He told us he was."

"He's a liar."

"He said that the two of you were in on a job together before you were caught."

NEWELL said grimly, "Bulkley is developing a sense of humor. What actually happened is that he framed me in order to shift the blame from himself. His plan worked only partially, and we were both convicted."

"Then this planet is a penal colony?"

"A substitute for one. In the old days—when crime was supposed to be common—I understand that the government maintained numerous penal colonies for convicted criminals, with psychiatrists to recondition the more promising colonies. But the last regular colony had been abandoned fifty years ago, and they didn't know what to do with us until some one hit on the idea of exiling us here. We were given all the supplies we could need, except those that would help us escape from the planet. And we began to have hope even of that when we discovered a spaceship that had been wrecked a long time before, and still had useful equipment."

The old man was staring around the plastex room. "Primitive, but apparently comfortable," he commented. His eyes fell on the brown and white creatures that were guarding them. "Those sir, I take it, are to he our permanent custodians. They appear to have distinct personalities."

"They look different," agreed Newell. "I'm hoping that I'll be able to work on them." His eyes came back to the girl. There was something about her that baffled him. Why had she turned red when he asked her whether she had special talents? And why was he so irritated by those unbecoming octagonal glasses, that silly hat, those stupidly ugly clothes?

He reached over, and with an abrupt motion lifted the glasses from her face. The transformation was striking. In the fraction of a second, she had become beautiful.

With no lenses to distort or conceal their expression, her eyes blazed. She sprang at him, and her hand stung his face. The two plant-guards, their light receptors responding to the sudden motion, wavered between him and the girl, their bodies quivering like trees in a storm of emotion. They had been conditioned to react to certain kinds of danger. But in a situation of this sort they did not know what to do.

NEWELL'S hand went to his face. You have a powerful swing," he said ruefully. "Isn't that unusual in a dancer?"

"So you know who I am…"

"Yes. Those glasses and those clothes were an effective disguise, but after a time your face did begin to seem annoyingly familiar. You did those exotic dances of Earth. Perhaps I'd have realized sooner if I had stopped to think that they were on film, just as your father's hypnotic tricks were. Somehow, however, I took it for granted that you were dancing in the studio."

"No, those dances were all recorded. I did them when I was working for my degree in Galactic Anthropology."

"What in space ever gave you the idea of wearing such clothes?"

"It was annoying to have people recognize me and turn to stare at me everywhere I went. It interfered with my getting new material."

"Maybe you don't know it, but Bulkley is a special fan of yours. He's been wanting to meet you for a long time."

"When I meet people like Bulkley, I always wear my glasses." She took them out of his hands and returned them to her face. He was amazed to see how completely they transformed her features back again. Now she was once more the dowdy woman of a few moments ago.

"At any rate," he said, "now I know what those special talents of yours are."

This time her expression was smooth, inscrutable. "You don't know the half of it," she said softly. "I have a surprise in store for your friend Bulkley."

Footsteps sounded outside. The door swung open, and Bulkley grinned at them. "Talking about me I imagine," he growled.

"Nothing good, of course," said Newell.

"I'll take care of you later, Newell. Meanwhile, we'd better get to work. I expect a visit from a patrol ship, and I want to be ready for it. You'll start at once to prepare those dragon-tooth seeds. I want them in a hurry. As for our guests, they'd better start building themselves a plastex hut. Unless, that is, Miss Hilton wants to move in with me."

"No, thank you," she said contemptuously.

"You don't realize how you're being honored. But if you won't accept, you don't have to...for now."

The old man was staring at him. Bulkley turned to him in some annoyance. "What in the galaxy are you looking at?"

"You, sir. I am attempting to estimate your intellectual and emotional strength."

He was trying to decide, realized Newell, whether Bulkley would be easy or difficult to hypnotize. It was a crucial question. For a time there was silence, as if all knew that they were weighing their future in the balance.

BULKLEY uttered an uneasy laugh. "You'll find that my strength is enough to keep you here. Just don't try any funny business."

"Of course not. As prisoner to captor, may I offer a suggestion, sir?"

"I don't want you to offer anything."

The old man nodded, as if pleased at the answer. "As I expected."

"What are you so happy about?"

"To find you so suggestible. If you will forgive an old pedagogue the weakness of indulging in his favorite vice of lecturing, I must impart this fact to you. There are two sorts of men who are extremely open to suggestion. The first kind adopts everything that is proposed to him."

"You'll find out that I'm not like that," said Bulkley.

"I have already done so, sir. You go to the opposite extreme. You *reject* everything—because you realize your own weakness. You put up artificial barriers to keep from doing as other people propose. You don't trust your own power of judgment to decide on what is good or bad. That means that once the barrier is crossed or broken, you will be at the mercy of the person who has broken it."

Newell found himself wondering. The old man was pompous in manner, vain of his ability, but he had the shrewdness of the centenarian. And now he might be right about Bulkley. Beneath the man's harsh brutality there might be a great lack of self-confidence. On the other hand the whole thing might be simply a lot of psychological double-talk, intended to break down Bulkley's powers of resistance.

Whatever it was, Bulkley didn't like it. He snarled, "I don't know what you're talking about. But I do know that you're of no use around here, and it wouldn't take me much to get rid of you altogether. Now get out, and start working on a plastex hut for yourself." He gestured to the side. "You'll find a foam gun in that closet."

Newell left the room, the two walking plants keeping close beside him. "There were possibilities, he thought, in the old man. He was testing Bulkley, probing for weak spots in the man's psychological make-up, without Bulkley's being aware of it. Unaided, he might not be able to hypnotize the murderer against his will, but with the proper apparatus, there were distinct possibilities of success. And now that Bulkley had to rely on them to prepare for the visit of the patrol ship, they might be able to make something that would be effective.

But Bulkley, they soon found, was not so stupid as to let any of his three captives lay hands on dangerous equipment. Newell tried to stall in various ways—he found a sudden need for chemicals or ultra flashlights at moments when Bulkley was busy with his own preparations. At such times, despite his desire for speed in the work, Bulkley made him wait. The proper chemicals or lights were used, and then removed to a spot where neither Newell nor his fellow captives could lay hands on them.

CHAPTER FOUR

BY THE END of the third day, after he had killed as much time as he dared, Newell had three thousand of the dragon-tooth seeds ready. That same night, the trouble that had been brewing finally erupted.

The pink sun was setting behind the trees, and the sky was quickly turning dark as Newell returned to the hut that he and Bulkley still shared, his guards dogging his footsteps as usual. Bulkley himself was not in sight. On the other side of the clearing stood the plastex hut, somewhat clumsily put together, that the old man had built for himself and his daughter.

Newell had seen little of the girl these past three days, although he had thought of her a great deal. There was irony in the thought that of all the women in the entire planetary system, she was the one that Bulkley had been the most eager to meet, although now that he had her practically in his grasp, he failed to recognize her.

Now, as Newell watched, the girl slipped out of her own hut and came toward his. Despite her deliberately unattractive clothes, she moved with the lithe grace of the trained dancer. If Bulkley had happened to see her at that moment, her walk alone might have given her away.

But apparently he was nowhere near, and she was able to gain the hut without interference. She came in, her plant-guards following her as they followed all of Bulkley's captives.

She began abruptly, "I wanted to talk to you. Alone."

He nodded. "Here's your chance."

"I don't know whether or not you were telling the truth about being framed. For all the evidence I have you're as much a criminal as Bulkley."

"What do I have to do to convince you that I'm not?"

"Nothing. You can't convince me. But it won't matter—at least, for a time. The main thing is that we've got to work together against him."

"Of course. Do you have a plan?"

"Father has. He says that Bulkley's so suggestible that if he had even the crudest hypnotic equipment he'd be able to control the man,"

"I've looked for equipment we could use. I've found nothing."

"Father suggested this television set. He might be able to use some of the transistors. Two would be enough."

"That's an idea. But suppose Bulkley comes in and decides to turn on the set?"

"That's a risk we'll have to take. Let's hope that we can hypnotize him before he discovers that something's wrong."

Newell walked over to the set, and opened it up. Quickly removing two of the tiny tubes, he put them in her hands. "Here they are. Tell your father to make use of them as soon as he can."

"Thank you."

"Tell him not to go to the trouble of hypnotizing me, though. Tell him that his daughter's eyes have already had that effect."

"You're rather suggestible yourself. How long is it since you've seen a woman on this planet?"

"A little over six months. But I haven't seen one like you in a lifetime."

"It's my clothes that attract you to me," she said sardonically.

HE DIDN'T answer in words. He saw a smile playing on her lips, and suddenly, moved by impulse, he pulled her to him, as if anxious to obliterate it with his own lips.

For a second or two she let him kiss her, then pushed him away. "Your friend is coming," she said simply.

Bulkley's footsteps were audible outside. He came in, saw them, and frowned. "When the cat's away, the mice will play," he said.

"I suppose so," she admitted coolly. "The old proverb seems fitting, although I've never seen a cat, and haven't the slightest idea what a mice is."

"*Mice* is plural. Singular mouse," explained Newell. "Once infested Earth, but could never adapt to other planets, and were eventually exterminated."

"Good idea, extermination," said Bulkley heavily. "I'd keep you, of course, sweetheart," he told her. "But I'm beginning to think I won't need Newell or your father anymore."

"You have a tendency to turn to murder to solve your problems, Bulkley," said Newell. "But this time I'm afraid you'd only complicate them. If you want more of those dragon's-teeth seeds, you'll have to keep me around."

"I wonder. You talk a little too much about murder, Newell. Almost as if you wanted to dare me. And our little schoolteacher friend here seems to be daring me in another way. I'd hate to disappoint her."

He put a rough hand on the girl's arm. Newell started toward him, only to find himself seized in the firm grip of two plant-creatures.

Bulkley said, "Take it easy, Newell. There's nothing you can do."

The girl said sharply, "Take your filthy paw off me."

That was the only encouragement a man like Bulkley needed. He laughed, and pulled her toward him.

What happened then amazed and startled Newell almost as much as it did the other man, although not so painfully. The great body of the man seemed to leap into the air and fly into the wall. He landed with a thud, and sank to the floor, dazed and half-unconscious.

Newell tried to leap forward toward the flashlight that had slipped from Bulkley's belt. But as he did so, the two plant creatures pulled him back. Rough twigs with bark-like surfaces tightened about his arms and held him helpless.

Despite his frustration, he had a feeling of elation, as if he had watched a miracle happen. How in the name of space had the girl done that to Bulkley?

Her expression was unruffled, and her lips were smiling again. "I told you I had other talents," she said.

"What diabolical trick was that?" asked Newell.

"One of the bits of knowledge I picked up while studying the ancient customs of Earth. It was known in its day as—let me see—jiu jitsu. The principles are simple enough, but the results are startling to a modern race that has long forgotten most of what it knew about physical combat."

Bulkley was picking himself up from the floor. Suddenly, as if he had convinced himself that what had happened to him the first time was only a bad dream, he rushed at her again.

THIS TIME he landed against the furniture and bounced off to the wall so violently that Newell hoped the man's skull was cracked.

"The greater the effort he makes, the harder he lands," explained the girl. "That's one of the beauties of jiu jitsu."

Bulkley's skull was a little too strong for plastex. He picked himself up, hesitated for a moment as if to attack again, then thought better of it. "Get back to your own hut," he told her hoarsely. "I'll attend to you later."

The girl left, her manner prim and dignified, the manner of a schoolteacher who has just given an unusually stupid pupil a lesson.

Bulkley glowered after her and then turned to face Newell. "Wipe that smile off your face," he ordered, in a rage.

"I wasn't smiling at you, my friend. I was just pitying you. You really were a pathetic sight."

"Keep your mouth shut, damn you!" roared the man.

"You'd better be careful from now on, Bulkley. That girl is dangerous. Too bad we don't have an X-ray machine here. You may have a serious concussion."

"I'm all right, and mind your own business." He turned to the television set and Newell realized that he intended to get his favorite program, hoping perhaps that Indra herself would appear. But the set did not light up.

"You probably smashed the insides when you landed against it," said Newell hastily. He stared into the set. "Whew! Everything's in a mess in here."

This time Bulkley cursed bitterly, emitting a long string of oaths that to Newell had novelty and interest, if not charm. Finally he turned away, and sank into his chair.

A little while later he went into his room, and dropped off to sleep.

But Newell stayed up. He thought for a while of the girl, and then of Bulkley, and what he could possibly do to free himself from the man's murderous grip. If only the plant-creatures were less alert! He was glad to see that they hadn't responded to the girl's motions when she had thrown Bulkley head over heels. That was probably because she had moved quite suddenly, and her motions had been on a small scale—the shift of weight from one foot then to another, the use of one arm for leverage, the other for a gentle push. If he moved like that, perhaps he would be able to put something over on them. He brooded for a long time, trying to find a way.

When finally he too went to sleep, he had made up his mind to wait for the right conditions, and then attempt a sudden dash for safety.

CHAPTER FIVE

It was the roar of an approaching spaceship that awoke them shortly before dawn. Newell and Bulkley rushed out of the hut, to stare up and see the faint white exhaust from the rocket tubes far off near the horizon against the fading blackness of the night.

The patrol ship, of course. The patrol ship that would try to cook Bulkley's goose. He would have to stay for a while.

The ship was coming down at a gentle slope, using the resistance of the atmosphere, as well as its own braking jets, to brake its fall. Its hull gleamed a low red from the heat of friction, then faded into pale gray, the shimmer of heat waves dancing around as it slowed down and made a gradual landing. It settled to the ground in a clearing half a mile from their own plastex hut.

Bulkley's eyes were glistening with anticipation. "That ship's all I need," he gloated. "I capture that and I get off the planet."

"You'll never get away with it," said Newell.

"No? You watch."

And because he had nothing better to do, Newell watched, with a gathering dread whose intensity grew from moment to moment.

DAWN WAS breaking. A door opened in the side of the ship and in the distance two men got out. The two tiny figures carried a heavy gun of some sort unknown to

Newell. This they mounted at the side of the ship, ready for any emergency—except for the one that actually threatened them!

Newell opened his mouth to yell a warning, and as he did so, Bulkley signaled an order with his flashlight. A wooden arm closed around Newell's throat and choked off his cry.

More men were getting off the ship. They moved cautiously, in pairs, and without suspicion of the real danger. They knew that two men had been left on the planet, and that one of them had attacked the freighter. But the planet itself was supposed to contain no wild beasts, no plants whose existence meant peril.

They could see about them now as the pink sun continued rising slowly over the horizon. What they saw seemed harmless—odd perhaps, but not threatening. Brown and white tree stumps stood rooted in the ground near the ship; branches lopped off in a most unusual fashion, so that stump after stump bore a great resemblance to a human scarecrow. They had never seen anything like these stumps before, but this was a new planet to them, and far stranger things were to be seen on other new planets.

With his flashlight, Bulkley shot an ultraviolet signal toward the ship. The captain was expecting no signals and paid no attention to the response of one of the instruments on his panel. But the brown and white scarecrows sprang into activity.

A pair of them leaped for the nearest gun, tore it from the grip of the startled patrolmen who had held it, and turned it on the ship itself. With the sound of firing, a shrill cry of alarm rang out. Terror awoke, and grew at the sudden attack.

The terrain around the ship became a field of battle. Men fell into the clutches of the plant-creatures and did not rise again. Those that survived the first onslaught raced back toward the ship.

Some of the plant-men were hit, too. Newell, the grip on his throat loosened now, could see them running around, their arms, legs, bodies in flames, their faces totally oblivious of such feelings and motions as pain and fear. The sight added the final touch of terror to the surprised patrol crew. Those already in the ship yelled to the others to close the door.

But it was already too late. The plant-creatures were inside the ship now, disregarding weapons fired at them point-blank, hunting down the survivors. Though their wooden bodies were torn and shattered, they were still capable of killing.

Bulkley was gloating, his eyes ablaze with the fervor of the despised man who sees his desperate plans working like a charm. "The ship's mine," he shouted. "Do you realize that, Newell? A complete spaceship, all mine. I can pack five hundred of my army into it and take them with me to the nearest planetary outpost; nothing will be able to stand before me."

He was right, thought Newell. The ship was his; the peaceful colonies on unprotected planets lay open to attack. Many a lone-wolf outlaw had dreamed of revenge on society for the wrongs he imagined he had suffered, for the punishments that the innocent had inflicted on him for his crimes. Yes, Bulkley was going to make these outlaw dreams come true.

The field of battle was empty of enemies now—the few human beings still on it were dead. Bulkley took a step forward.

And the planet shook.

THE GROUND rocked and trembled under foot like a vast heap of jelly. They could feel the vibrations from some distant slide of rock strata. In the forest ahead of them a row of trees suddenly tipped over, as if toppled by a giant hand.

Bulkley fell, his flashlight flying away from him. Newell, dropping to all fours for his own safety, made a lunge for the flashlight, his fingers closing about it. Bulkley did not notice him.

The plant-creatures had reacted in an unexpected way. Their foot-like appendages became rooted in the ground, held them firm. The wind was rising now, and as sudden gusts came blustering down upon them, they bent before it, springing up again when the pressure was released.

It was useless to try to use the lights upon them now. Newell did not know the combinations of wave lengths to which they responded, and the stimuli from the wind were now so strong as to control their movements; He saw Bulkley rise and turn to him, to shout a few words which the wind carried away, and then take a step toward him.

The ground between the two men opened up. A gulf suddenly yawned between them, a dozen feet wide and a hundred deep. Newell knew from previous experience that the earthquakes were violent, but that the series of shocks was of short duration. In a few moments, Bulkley would recover his wits, and regain control of the plant-creatures. If there was a chance to escape, Newell would have to take it now.

He tried to run, but the wind, now of hurricane force, knocked him down, and he crawled as fast as he could over the heaving ground. He could hear nothing but the howling of the wind, and up above streamers shot out of the sun, while the great disk of the flaming star itself grew dark and gloomy as the vast clouds of dust rose into the air and obscured the light.

He reached the rows of fallen trees, and began to crawl over the tops of them.

Suddenly, as suddenly as it had begun, the earthquake ended. The ground grew firm beneath the fallen trees, the heaving, as of a ship in a violent storm, came to an end. The wind still blew, but not quite with its former force. From second to second he could feel how its strength subsided. Only the clouds of dust still obscured the sun, which he knew from past experience would not regain its brightness for at least a day.

He sank down among the trees. Bulkley would soon be looking for him, desperate because of his need for more dragon-tooth seeds, more soldiers. The seeds that Newell had already prepared would not sprout, as Newell well realized, and the other man's rage would be something fearful to behold.

In the distance Newell could see the two plastex huts, their sides cracked and twisted. Well, that damage amounted to little. Plastex powder could be poured into the cracks for repairs, and a twisted hut, although novel in design, was just as good a shelter as one with straight sides.

But the ship—and then he realized why he could see so far ahead of him. The ship had sunk into the ground, which had opened beneath the great hull and then closed again with the power of a gigantic nutcracker. The metal hull was shattered now shattered beyond hope of repair. It was the same thing that had happened to the other spaceship long before Newell and Bulkley had arrived on the planet.

He could hear the sound of Bulkley's cursing. The man could not get off the planet now. He would have to wait for another patrol ship to come searching for the first one. His plans would have to be delayed. And for Newell, delay meant hope.

Bulkley would, he knew, send his plant-creatures to search for him from the moment the man recovered from the immediate effects of the disaster. Newell had to get further away. Only distance meant safety.

HE BEGAN to make his way through the trees, when unexpectedly the sound of human speech came to his ears.

He swung around. Indra was helping her father over a fallen tree trunk. They too had escaped. Bulkley was without human companionship now, alone with his army of plant-soldiers. And he was more desperate and more dangerous than ever.

The old man saw him, and a smile broke over the old withered face. Now there was somebody else besides the old gentleman's daughter to talk to. "Ah, my dear sir," began Hilton. "I am pleased to see that you too have escaped. It is an ill wind that blows no good."

"This wind didn't do half the damage the earthquake did."

"And those creatures." The girl shuddered. "The slaughter was sickening. I had to turn my eyes away."

"The slaughter will be repeated with the next patrol ship," said Newell soberly. "Unless we find a way to stop it."

The old pedagogue shrugged. "It was very difficult even under the previous conditions, as you well realize, Mr. Newell, to get at Bulkley. It will be doubly difficult now that we have escaped. He will undoubtedly post guards to watch for us."

"We'll have to think of ways of getting past them. How is that hypnotic device of yours coming along?"

"Ah, I had almost forgotten. Thank you, sir, for reminding me. The fact is that it is coming along, to use your phrase. Indeed, it is completed. It has not, however, undergone actual test, so I cannot vouch for its effectiveness." From his pocket he pulled out what seemed like a short blunt plastex tube. "Observe."

Newell stared at the end of the tube. He could see it begin to glow dully, turn cherry red, orange, white, and then orange and red again. The next time it raced through the spectral gamut of colors from red to violet, faded out, and seemed to retrace its steps. And all the time its intensity ebbed and flowed, ebbed and flowed, as pulses of energy raced one after the other through the short tube.

He was tired, Newell realized, tired of the horrifying excitement of the battle. He would like to get away from everything, forget the planet, forget Bulkley, and forget the plant-creatures. He would like to rest, to sleep.

His head snapped back, and he was suddenly alert. "Take that thing away!" he shouted.

The old man chuckled with satisfaction. "Indeed, sir. This is more effective than I had thought. The combination of color change and intensity fluctuation makes it difficult for most people to resist. The exact rhythm is, of course, of great importance. It is the result of a great many experiments, a great deal of work and thought for which I, sir, cannot claim a particle of credit. The principle was first discovered by a professor of a distant system—"

"Never mind that, Mr. Hilton. The main thing is that it works."

"Yes, it is, as I say, rather effective, even when used without the adjust of suggestion. If, in addition, sleep-suggestive words or, on occasion, syllables are employed, successful hypnosis is almost guaranteed. If you are one of those unfortunate sufferers from insomnia, troubled sleep, inability to relax..."

For the first time that morning Newell found something to laugh at. "You don't have to go into your Dr. Hypno spiel," he said. "I'll take your word for it that it works."

THE OLD man fondled the hypnotic device like a child with his toy. "I am rather anxious now," he said, "to get a chance to use this on Bulkley."

"Later, Father, later," his daughter told him, and the old man smiled and seemed to become absent-mindedly lost in his own thoughts, as he wandered away from them into the forest.

Newell turned to the girl, noticing now that in her haste to escape she hadn't managed to make herself as unattractive as usual. Her clothes fitted the lithe body more snugly and disturbingly. Looking at her now, you could believe that she was the dancer who had appeared on television and aroused the enthusiasm of the inhabitants of an entire planetary system.

But her own mind did not seem to be on her appearance. She was in a serious mood as she said, "We can't stay out here in the woods for long."

"You mean because of your father."

"Yes. He's only a hundred and twenty, but he's not in good health. And if the weather should turn bad..."

"You needn't worry about the weather here. It's mild all year round, and there's little rain. It's the wind that's dangerous. Even when there are no earthquakes, it sometimes rises to hurricane force, and the falling trees would be deadly."

"We'll have to find a cleared space."

"And we'll have to watch out for those plant-creatures. Bulkley may send them out looking for us."

He thought she looked troubled, but he could not read the expression in her eyes behind the lenses. Once more he reached toward her and lifted the octagonal glasses from her face. This time she did not slap him.

"You don't really need those," he said.

"They've just became a habit," she admitted.

"Meant to keep people at a distance. But you don't need them with me. You have your jiu jitsu."

"Yes, I can always fall back on that."

"I suppose I risk being thrown head over heels if I so much as try to kiss you."

"I'm sure that you realize that it's happened to others before you."

"It's a risk that's worth taking."

He was not thrown head over heels. But when he let go of her, his brain was in such a whirl that he felt almost as if he had been.

CHAPTER SIX

BULKLEY sent his plant-slaves after them that very day, a few hours before the sun was due to set. It was hard at first to see the creatures coming, for their brown and white surfaces blended all too perfectly with the natural browns and whites and greens of their parent forest. But when they moved forward, they became visible. And soon Newell could see them, from twenty-five to fifty of them, scattered in a long thin row and marching straight ahead, slowly, giving a terrifying impression of implacable power.

"What do we do?" whispered the girl. "We can't fight them."

"I know one thing we can do to beat them off. But it'll take time. Meanwhile, we run. They can't move fast enough to catch us."

"But my father is too old!"

"He won't have to race along. We have a head start, and if we keep going steadily, a fast walk will do. The important thing is to keep the distance between us and them, and to add to it."

They turned and began to crash through the forest. The old man grumbled, at first. Running away was beneath his dignity. He would face these creatures and stand on his rights, explain to them that what they were doing was illegal and would be punished.

NEWELL did not wait to hear what else the old man wanted to say. He simply dragged the unwilling pedagogue along and, soon, lack of breath forced his companion to stop talking.

They had been moving for an hour, more at a fast walk than at a run, when a slight wind arose. It was cool and pleasant, and blew in their faces so refreshingly that at first Newell did not think of what it might mean to his plans. When he realized how it could help, he came to a stop.

There were dead and dried trees scattered all through the forest, and inside them he found the tinder he needed. The flashlight he had taken from Bulkley had tiny permanent batteries that were capable of giving a strong spark. It was the work of but a moment to set fire to the tinder, and to nurse the tiny flame until it grew fierce and ravenous.

Using a flaming branch, he spread the fire through the forest. The wind, blowing steadily, spread the blaze into a continuous sheet, and urged it forward. The sound of crackling branches became a steady roar, a roar that rose louder and louder as it seized upon new fuel. The sheet of flame swept on, driven by the wind, and accompanied by the fierce crescendo music that its own fury aroused.

Into the flames walked the plant-creatures. Theirs not to reason why, theirs but to do and die.

They died.

Newell could see some of them, animate torches stalking through a sea of flame. They moved forward as long as they could, and when the flames had seized them too completely, they toppled over and finished burning on the ground.

There was something to be said after all, he thought, for human beings, with all their fears and imperfections. The very fact that they had reason to live made them worse soldiers under conditions where sacrifices were needed.

But sometimes sacrifices were stupid and in vain. Sometimes the best thing a soldier could do for his own cause was to be afraid, and keep himself alive. And that kind of wisdom the plant-creatures did not have.

Indra looked troubled. "They seem so—so human," she said. "I know they're not, but all the same, I felt as if I were watching human beings walk to their deaths."

He nodded somberly. "I feel the same way. But Bulkley doesn't. To him their lives are meaningless as the lives of so many blades of grass. That's where he has the advantage over us."

"And he has almost two thousand more in reserve?"

"Almost. A few were killed in the attack on the ship, and more have just been burned, but he still has the greater part of his slave army." Sudden rage seized him at the thought. "The army that I provided for him."

"No use worrying about it now. Father seems tired and can't run any further. Let's think of shelter for the night."

He shook his head impatiently. "There's something else to do, and I'm the only one who can do it. You find a place for yourself and your father to sleep if you want to. I'm setting to work."

"What do we do for food?"

"I'll show you which plants are edible." He pointed out a small bush. "You can collect these berries. They're tasty and nourishing. If you want to, you can collect a meal for me, after you yourself have eaten. In the meantime, the only thing you can give me is inspiration."

She eluded his arms. "No. I don't want you to forget your work."

He *would* have forgotten it, he told himself. Now that he knew her better, he realized that she could make him forget anything but herself.

He put the thought aside, and began to collect the seeds be needed. Equipment he could improvise. And most of the necessary chemicals he'd be able to extract from the same kinds of plants he had used before.

SOON HE was so lost in his work that it came as a shock of surprise when she appeared before him with berries to eat. He ate mechanically, hardly aware of the taste of the food.

"What are you doing?" she asked.

"Fighting fire with fire—another kind of fire. Trying to create a slave army of my own."

"How long before they're ready?"

"Two days to prepare the seeds, another day for them to grow, and for the plant creatures to undergo preliminary training."

"Suppose Bulkley finds us before then?"

"Then we're out of luck. The fact is, even if he doesn't find us, I'll have to go looking for danger. I don't have all the chemicals I need. One complex compound is in a vial, in what's left of our plastex hut. I'll have to go back for it."

"That's insane! You'll never be able to get away with it."

"I'll have to try."

She had turned pale, and Newell thought with surprise, "She's worried about me. Is it because she's counting on me to protect her against Bulkley—or is it something deeper?"

She said, "I'll go with you. Two will stand a better chance than one."

"No. You'd only distract me. I'd be thinking of your safety instead of my own."

"I want to help you. In any way you say. I can help you prepare your chemicals."

He shook his head doubtfully. "That requires careful work."

"I can do careful work. I've done experiments in chemical science. Have you forgotten that I'm a schoolteacher?"

He looked at her. The effort to escape through the forest from the pursuing plant-creatures had torn her once ill-fitting clothes in many places, and lent them a casual charm they had not originally possessed. There were rips through which he could see her body, and it was not the kind of body he thought of as belonging to a schoolteacher. Doubtless, he was doing schoolteachers an injustice.

"Good thing you reminded me," he grunted. And he turned back to his labors.

CHAPTER SEVEN

Thanks to her help, it was evening of the following day, sooner than he had expected, when he retraced his path toward the plastex hut that he had shared for six months with the man who now wanted to kill him.

He had a weapon—the hypnotizer that Indra's father had fashioned. It was much less reliable than a gun, but it was the best he could get, and it would have to do. If he was lucky, he would avoid Bulkley altogether, and not have the chance to use it. But if Bulkley discovered him trying to steal that vial of chemicals...

He shrugged. There would be trouble, and all the advantages would be on the other man's side. He must avoid discovery as long as he could.

He made his way cautiously through the forest in the darkness, not daring to use his flashlight. He knew, even before his feet crunched the charred wood, when he had reached the burned-out portion of the forest. The odor of burned wood was overpowering. And here and there, after more than twenty-five hours, sparks still glowed in the night, like tiny signal fires lighting his way.

After the burned forest was behind him, he became even more cautious. Bulkley, he knew, now that the man was alone, would be sleeping with the lightness and insecurity of a feral beast, ready to start up at any noise. The plant-creatures were not very sensitive to slight sounds, not unless they had been conditioned to detect sounds more thoroughly than Newell imagined was possible. But with light-receptors scattered all over their surfaces, they had an extraordinary sensitiveness to light. The merest alteration of dim light to faint shadow, or vice versa, might arouse them.

ONCE A TWIG snapped under his feet, and he came to a halt. But in the army of resting plant-creatures, all was quiet, and after a tense thirty seconds he went on again, more carefully this time, testing the ground with each foot before he let his weight fall upon it. A hundred yards to one side he was aware of a darker shadow, of a great mass that was even blacker than the surrounding black. It was the smashed hull of the spaceship, won by ruthless slaughter, and wrecked in a moment of giant and more ruthless playfulness by the planet itself. Now only the top protruded above the level of the surrounding soil.

As he approached the hut, he dropped to the ground and crawled. The less possibility of casting a shadow, he told himself, the better. Walking was more convenient, but also more dangerous. He crawled, slowly and painfully.

He was at the door of the hut. Quiet reigned, a dead absence of sound held sway. No...there was a sound— something low and menacing, something...

I'm a damn fool, he thought. *It's my own breathing.*

He held his breath, and heard through the walls of the hut the faintest of sighs. Now it was Bulkley's breathing he heard, the breathing of a Bulkley who slept untroubled, with no murderous dreams to disturb his rest, no fear of danger to himself.

Newell figured there must be plant-creatures on guard—some of them must be present in the hut itself. But the hut was dark. Lucky for Newell that they weren't very sensitive to heat radiations, a fact that had been established with the television set parts. Newell didn't want his body heat to set them off. But they were sensitive to the near-visible infrared, and visible light, and ultraviolet. For plants, they were unusually sensitive. But they needed a stimulus in order to respond. No stimulus, no response. If they didn't see Newell, if not so much as a single photon set off their light-receptors, he would be safe.

Inside the hut Newell's thoughts were racing. *Stop again, listen again—Bulkley's breathing is louder now. I can hear it almost like an intermittent roar when I hold my own breath, but there's no other change. If only I don't touch a plant-creature in the dark. I know where the chemical is that I want. I can feel my way around without switching on a light, as I did for so many months when I lived here. Bulkley may have made changes in the past few days, but he hasn't changed the location of the closet. Ah, here it is. I reach inside. Here are the bottles, large and small. I don't need to read the labels to know what's inside them. Acids, indole derivatives—ah, here's the vial I want. I know its size, its shape. All I need now is a single crystal, but common sense dictates that I take it all. I may need more later, and besides, there's no sense leaving anything for Bulkley to use.*

Theft mission accomplished safely—or almost, anyway. Now to get away from here.

Unexpectedly there was a noise. A noise not from the hut itself, but from overhead. A faint drone like that of some insect zooming through the air, preparing for a dive, at the end of which it would dip its tiny jaws into human skin for a meal of blood. The drone became a roar—the roar of a spaceship. Another patrol vessel, of course, had come to see what had happened to its predecessor. More cautious than the first one, scanning the planet for danger before landing, with no desire to come down in the dark. Its crew was being very smart, laudably smart. But helpless for all its smartness and all its caution, because its captain and its crew didn't realize the real danger, didn't realize that death might come from the seemingly harmless plants with which the surface of the planet was covered.

STILL, caution kept the ship safe for the moment. The roar died away to a faint drone again, to silence again, as the visitors scouted the planet. Newell hoped they didn't find them too soon.

He hoped it for their sake.

There wasn't a sound now. Not even the sound of Bulkley's breathing. Newell thought, *That's odd. Very odd. A man asleep breathes deeply, heavily...*

But Bulkley wasn't asleep. Bulkley was standing in the doorway of his room, a flashlight in one hand, a weapon in the other. Bulkley grinned evilly at him, ready to shoot, ready to kill.

Newell thought, *Wish to amend previous report. Theft mission* not *accomplished safely.*

Bulkley moved forward. "Don't move, Newell," he cautioned. "Not unless you want to die in a hurry."

Newell froze. *That damned spaceship*, he thought to himself bitterly. *Cautious as all space itself. So cautious that it woke him up.*

The flashlight went off as the room lights went on. Bulkley said comfortably, "Sit down. Be comfortable. Make yourself at home. Make believe you live here."

Humor from Bulkley, of all people. Or was it just humor? The place was home, the house was still as comfortable as ever, but that wasn't the reason Bulkley wanted him to sit. A sitting man couldn't leap at you with the suddenness that a standing man could. A sitting man was like a sitting duck, easy to keep under the muzzle of your own weapon, and Newell's weapon of surprise had been taken away from him.

"Thought you'd be back, Newell.   Thought you wouldn't want to leave your old pal without saying goodbye.   And you're not getting away again.   I don't expect another earthquake soon, but if there is one, I'll shoot you dead at the first sign of it."

HE'LL SHOOT me anyway when he has no more use for me. What do I do now? Those plant-creatures are watching me. Three of them here with us in the room. Strange to think that they were here all the time, like dummies, hearing nothing, seeing nothing, doing nothing. Tough-Egg and Kind-Mugg—I recognize them. Or are these their twins? Could be. The third one looks even more human. A brown scar with white trimmings down a brown and white face. Scar-face. Human and sinister.

Never mind how they look. It's how they act that counts. They act like robots, perfect robots under Bulkley's control. Well, not perfect, perhaps. They have their weaknesses. But none that I can count on. The question is: What do I do now?

Nothing with them directly. Can't think of a thing to do. Bulkley is very likely the real weak link in the chain that's got me trapped. Settle his hash, and the robots are left without orders, they're harmless. Yes, put Bulkley out of commission for a few seconds, and you get a start. And given that start, you can outrun them, especially in the dark.

Let's start off. My hand can slip casually along the arm of the plastex chair in which I'm sitting. Bulkley notices nothing wrong. Good. The thing now is to talk, talk heatedly, passionately—talk in any way that will arouse Bulkley's interest, get him excited, not let him see what that hand is going to do. The hand is going to be quicker than the distracted eye. The hand is going to slip into a pocket and pull out the hypnotizer. The pulsing light will glow and change color, and then Bulkley's eyes will be drawn to it, and then before he realizes what it is and what it's doing to him..."

"All right, Bulkley, you've got me. What do you want of me?"

"First thing I want you to help me get that girl back."

"That schoolteacher? Thought you didn't like her."

"School-teacher in a space-devil's eye. She's that dancer. I had her in my hands and didn't realize it. Just last night I was watching that program—yes, I fixed the television set, my friend, and found that some of the parts were missing. But anyway, I was watching the program, and it struck me that I had seen her face before."

"Quick on the trigger. That's you, Bulkley."

"I'm the one who's in a position to be funny, Newell, not you."

"Sure, sure...you're a born humorist."

He's beginning to burn. Fine. He isn't watching my hand at all.

"I'm warning you for the last time, Newell. Don't try to be funny. I want that girl back."

Laugh at him. Laugh when you want to smash his face.

"You're crazy, Bulkley. Or is it your turn to try to be funny?"

"I'm not crazy and I'm not funny. I want her back."

"You heard me. The answer is, 'No'."

The man's eyes are glittering. Hope I don't carry this too far. Don't want him to shoot.

Bulkley's lips seemed to be dry. He licked them before speaking. "You're a fool, Newell. A complete fool. What's the girl to you? You've known her for only a couple of days. She means nothing to you. She can't possibly mean anything. And whether you live or die, sooner or later I'll get her anyway. I'm offering you your life if you help me get her now."

"You're wasting your time." *Wrong tactics, here. I should stall, ask him what he wants me to do. But I can't. Not on a subject like this. To hell with even thinking of stalling on a subject like this.* "If this is the subject you want to talk about. Shoot me and get it over with. I won't discuss it."

THAT stopped him. Bulkley's face was red with anger and frustration. He said evenly, "Whatever I decide to do to you, Newell, it won't be the way you want it to be. I won't shoot you and just get it over with. That would be pleasant for you. But I don't like to cut my own pleasures short that way. For a time, at least, I'm going to keep you alive."

"You can't keep me alive against my will. Try to torture me, and I'll kill myself. And I'll take you with me."

"You tempt me, Newell." The words were slow, weighed carefully. "I hesitate to tell you how much you tempt me. I've hated your guts ever since I've known you—"

"Ever since you framed me. We always hate those we hurt. Sense of guilt, I suppose."

"You're wrong. I don't feel guilty about what I've done to you. I'm only sorry it wasn't worse. And I'm going to do all I can to make it worse."

"Aren't you overlooking something, Bulkley? We're not going to be alone on this planet much longer. That was a spaceship that woke you."

"I know that. I heard it."

"Isn't that going to interfere with your plans? Some place out there..." His left arm gestured vaguely toward vaguely toward the window. "...that ship will be landing soon. The captain and the crew know that something is wrong with this planet. That's why they came in such a hurry to search for the first ship. They'll be careful, this time. You won't catch them by surprise again."

"You're a fool." Contempt was in Bulkley's voice. "They can't be careful enough, because they don't realize what they have to be careful about. What ship ever worries about being attacked by trees?"

He was right and Newell knew it, but he couldn't let him know that he agreed with him. "They'll be suspicious of everything."

"No…they won't be suspicious of the one thing they should suspect."

Like you, my friend. You're watching to make sure that I don't try to leap at you from this chair. But you're not suspicious of the vague gesture I make with my left arm. You don't realize that your eyes follow it without your meaning them to, and that while your attention is distracted toward the window, my right hand has slipped into a pocket and drawn out the hypnotizer.

Now to start it going—low power, at first, so that you don't even realize the light's on. Low power, and in the near-visible infrared, so that your eyes begin to be affected without your actually seeing anything. You're susceptible to suggestion, the old man proved that when he first spoke to you in my presence. Before you know it, your eyes will be glazed; you won't be able to tear them away. You'll do as I tell you, and all your desperate plans will end in failure.

Mustn't look at the light myself, though. I know what it can do. I'll resist it if my eyes do happen to glance at it, but still it's best not to take chances. Fine joke it would be if I were hypnotized myself. Turn the power up a bit, slowly, gradually, so he doesn't even realize the light is visible…

Bulkley was talking abruptly. Words meant little now, but Newell had to pretend to listen.

"However, that space thing isn't the thing I want to talk about. I'll handle it when the time comes. And then there won't be another earthquake to crush it, and I'll have a ship I can use to get off this damned planet."

"So you think."

"That's the way it'll be. But how about you, Newell? Do you want to live or die? Or maybe that isn't the question. Because after I start working on you I know that you'll want to die, even if I decide to let you live. The real question is whether you'll do it the easy way, or insist on suffering a little first."

"Let's be reasonable, Bulkley." *Just a moment of reason, before the thing has him under control.* "I don't like to be tortured any more than the next man. But what you're asking—"

"Cut it out, Newell."

THERE'S something unexpected in the man's voice. Something I don't understand and don't like. There's a sneer of brutal triumph, an overwhelming tone of contempt. Have I made a fool of myself?

"What do you mean, cut it out?"

"Stop stalling for time. Because that thing you have in your hand isn't working. And it isn't going to work, no matter how long you keep it going. I'm not susceptible to hypnotizers."

Impossible. He's lying, trying to upset me. The dirty rat is wide open to suggestion. The hypnotizer will work in ninety-nine cases out of a hundred even on the average man, and there's no reason why it shouldn't affect him.

Bulkley was laughing. "There are a few things about me that you didn't know, Newell. I never thought of telling them to you. When I was under investigation, they also figured, as I knew they would, that I'd be susceptible to suggestion, and they tried to hypnotize me. But I was way ahead of them. I pretended to let myself go, but told them nothing, absolutely nothing."

"But how—"

"Because I can't be hypnotized." Triumph was in his brutal voice again. "I'm immune to it, at least when tried by any ordinary man or with any ordinary device. You immunize yourself against bacterial infection, viral infection—well, I immunized myself against hypnotism long ago. I went to a specialist who got me under control, and then gave me this posthypnotic suggestion: *Never let yourself be hypnotized again.* Clever trick for a murderer, isn't it, Newell? And the suggestion's still working."

He's outwitted me. Let him gloat, he has a right to do it. Crude, murderous, brutal—he's also got a kind of shrewdness I hadn't counted on. He's made a complete fool of me. And the cost—the cost is not only my own life, which doesn't count any more, but Indra's, her father's...

THE SIGHT of his desperate face must have been funny. Bulkley chose that moment to laugh again—and within the fraction of a second, the very strength of desperation had, sent Newell leaping out of his chair, his hands reaching straight for the man's throat.

Bulkley's arm went up instinctively in a gesture of self-protection, and a hoarse cry came from his lips. "Help!"

The plant-creatures didn't move. Newell's hands missed the throat, balled into fists, and smashed at the other man's jaw. Bulkley staggered backward and fell. And still his once faithful slaves did not come to his help. Tough-Egg, Kind-Mugg, Scar-Face, all three stood as if paralyzed—no, as if hypnotized. The hypnotizer, which had failed on Bulkley, had succeeded with them!

Bulkley cursed, and his hand went to the weapon at his side. Newell threw a chair at him. The chair landed, but did not knock the weapon from his hand. Newell raced for the door, and plunged through just as a blast tore a hole through the wall behind him.

He was running in the darkness now, his hypnotizer still glowing. It made him a target for Bulkley, but he had to risk it, now that he knew what it could do to the plant-creatures. He should have suspected what would happen. They reacted in different ways to different light stimuli. When the lights followed one another in rapid succession, as they did in the hypnotizer, they were stimulated to do different, contradictory things. The result was that they did nothing, standing motionless like the plants from which they had descended.

Bulkley was pursuing him in the darkness. A blast came, ripping a hole of flame in the night before the darkness overwhelmed it again. And then Newell ducked behind a genuine tree, and Bulkley could no longer see the glow of light, could no longer follow. Newell heard his curses die away in the distance.

He paused for a moment to catch his breath before going ahead.

CHAPTER EIGHT

He told Indra of his narrow escape, he could see how strongly she was affected. Her face paled; her voice shook.

"He'll be murderous now," she shuddered. "He'll come after you, do anything to revenge himself on you."

"He may send the plant-creatures after us. But now we can defend ourselves from them with the hypnotizer, and Bulkley knows that. He'd have to come himself if he really wanted to get us."

"He knows that in the long run we can't escape. Father can't run far. And I wouldn't leave him to Bulkley's mercy."

"But Bulkley doesn't have the time to spare for us. Don't you see, Indra, he has to be ready for that spaceship. He doesn't know where it will land, and he can't take chances with it. It may blast a cleared space among the trees and come down among them. And then the sight of his plant-creatures, no matter how much they imitate other trees, will arouse suspicion. Bulkley has to arrange his soldier-slaves beforehand, give them signals as to what to do."

"So you think we're safe for a while?"

"Until the spaceship comes down and is attacked."

"But we can't let those crew men be slaughtered the same way the others were. We have to do something!"

"What?"

"Warn them, signal them—"

"Not so long as they're up in the air. We don't have the proper equipment for that. Besides, they'll be suspicious of whoever contacts them. If we did try to signal them too soon, they'd be wary of us, not of Bulkley. No, the best thing we can do is plan to reach the ship after it comes down, and spoil Bulkley's surprise."

"You mean to use the hypnotizer?"

"It should be helpful."

"But suppose Bulkley realizes that," she pointed out. "He'll try to recondition his creatures. You say that he himself foresaw that attempts would be made to hypnotize him, and took steps against it. Suppose he finds a way to protect those plant-creatures against hypnosis?"

Newell nodded slowly. "You're right, Indra, there's that danger. I can't laugh it off. I've been underestimating Bulkley all along, but I mustn't underestimate him now. That might be fatal..."

"If we had such a thing as a flame-thrower—"

"We haven't. But talking about flame-throwers reminds me, Indra. As I said before, we have to fight fire with fire. And slaves with slaves. I'm almost ready to do so now."

He pulled from his pocket the vial that he had gone to so much trouble to obtain. "We'll have to go ahead with our experiments, as fast as we can. I'll work through the night to get the dragon-tooth seeds ready for planting."

"How about the field to plant them in?"

"That has to be prepared too. It won't take long to make the proper chemical solutions for that, though. And you can help me."

"Aren't you glad now that I'm a schoolteacher and have such good ideas?"

HE HELD her in the darkness and laughed. "I didn't fall in love with you for your ideas."

"You're like any other man. You fall in love for the worst reasons. Because to you I was a pretty face on a television screen…"

"Not only a face."

"Don't make me blush."

"Blush? You're still a schoolteacher after all. Put on your glasses and get to work."

The planet had no moon, but during the night the sky cleared, and the starlight poured down upon them, bright, clear, and cool. Newell switched off the flashlight, which he had been using from time to time as he mixed his chemicals, and went ahead with his work in the semi-darkness. Indra worked near him, and the thought of her, so close that he was aware of her every movement, sent a warm thrill through him. No wonder Bulkley envied him and went mad with rage when he thought of Newell's good fortune.

He was within a few minutes of completing his work when the new day dawned. Indra's father had been sleeping a short distance away on a heap of leaves that his daughter had carefully collected and made up into a soft bed. Now he arose, somewhat stiffly, and shook both the drowsiness and the leaves from him.

"These are indeed primitively simple surroundings for a man of a hundred and twenty-one," he commented. "And I do not believe that sleeping on the ground is favorable to the condition of my joints. No, indeed, I regard that as a most injudicious proceeding, although, in the circumstances, inevitable. Nevertheless, sir, I imagine that the overall effect is rather invigorating. There is nothing like direct contact with nature to restore the energy of the human psyche."

Newell, too busy with his work to have time for small talk, grunted.

"It is gratifying to know, sir, that you are in agreement with me. It is living in this manner that gives promise for the future of humanity. I sometimes am inclined to believe, Mr. Newell, that our present mode of existence is too complicated, too confusing. It baffles the soul, deprives it of contact with true cosmic greatness. Yes, I fear that we have lost contact with the true Truth, we have been deprived of the simplicity that once was ours. We dwell in great cities, on amazing planets that are parts of great systems. We go, in the happy and carefree days of youth, to great nurseries, and then to great schools, great universities. We enter upon great and difficult duties. It was different, in the old days."

Old men weren't any different, though, thought Newell. Wonder if they could talk quite as well as that. When you listened to that rich resonant voice and didn't pay too much attention to the meaning, you might actually think he was saying something different. So times have changed—imagine thinking that was a great discovery!

But that voice—no wonder the old boy's a good hypnotist. The very way he thinks is calculated to put you to sleep. Fuzzy mind, furry voice—wonder if they had any quite as good as him then, always looking back with regret to *their* old days.

"My father, sir, lived to a hundred and sixty-three, and even then it was only accident that ended his life. I was born when he was one hundred and eleven. I come from a long-lived line, sir, a line that retains its manly powers for many years."

"Boasting, huh? Okay, Pop, go ahead."

Indra must have heard him. "Father," she called.

"Yes, dear?"

"I know that Mr. Newell is too polite and too considerate to ask you but we are doing something in a hurry—"

"An enterprise of great moment, eh, dear?"

"Yes, it's important. It would be very nice if you could help."

"Anything within the limits of my abilities, Indra, dear, anything within the rather wide limits of my abilities. Tell me your difficulties, and I shall do my best to counsel you properly."

"You don't understand, Father. We don't need advice. We'll tell you what to do."

The old throat cleared. "Unfortunately, Indra, as you know, I lack the abounding physical energies that once were mine. Mentally I am as alert as ever, but physically…

"It won't be difficult, Father."

"One moment, Indra. I must tell Mr. Newell something. Would you believe it, sir, when I was twenty-three and a student at the Intermediate—no, at the Lesser Galactic Graduate School-Section 4A—or was it 5C? —let me see, now—"

"Here, Father," said Indra coaxingly. "It's really very simple. It's a matter of digging furrows, as we sometimes see in the pictures that have come down to us from primitive times."

"Such menial labor as that, eh, daughter?" But he went over to her, and Indra, to Newell's surprise, soon had him doing useful work.

Newell shook his head to get all those words out of his ears, and then went on with his own work. Unexpected difficulties had cropped up.

The sun was two hours above the horizon when he finally began to plant the dragon-tooth seeds.

IT WENT slower here than when he had first planted them. This was no cleared field where he could stride without watching his footsteps. This was a partial clearing at best, the path broken by trees, stumps, and bushes of all kinds. But there had been no time to seek for better ground. This would have to do to raise a crop of the dragon-tooth creatures.

The girl and the old man watched in awe as the shoots began to push their way up. Now, as the growing plants became gradually more human in appearance, there was no effect as of an army of men springing into existence. Each plant-creature was surrounded by other plants, so that as the young shoots grew they appeared to be merely coming out of a hiding place which they had assumed long before.

"Remarkable," said the old man. "A most remarkable phenomenon. Still, it is not absolutely unprecedented. I recall the descriptions of some of the plant-beasts of the lesser known stars…"

"Of course, Father." Indra turned to Newell. "How do you handle them now?"

"With lights. It isn't going to be easy. I have my flashlight, and I have the glow of the hypnotizer. I'll have to condition them to signals of different intensity and different rhythms. They exhibit a natural tropism—a tendency to move—toward red light and away from violet. It's doubtless connected with the pinkness of the sun. At any rate, that helps me to control their movements, and at the same time, gives me a chance to combine the light signals with loud vocal commands, condition them to respond to words."

"Doesn't that take a great deal of time?"

"I should be able to get good results in a few hours."

Up above, there was the same roar he had heard the preceding night. The sun glinted on a tiny silvery shape before distance shrank the ship to an undetectable point.

"That's the spaceship that came last night!" she exclaimed.

"They're still cruising around, trying to find Bulkley and me. I hope they don't succeed in spotting the plastex huts too soon."

"But surely, now that they know something has happened to the first ship, they won't be so easy to rake by surprise…"

He shook his head. "I'm not counting on them. They know about the earthquakes that occur here, and if they come across the ruins of the first ship, caught in the ground, they may think at first that the ship was the victim of an accident. Bulkley might even take steps to make them think that. He might, for instance, put up a signal of distress."

"Then we don't have too much time."

"Right. The sooner I can get my soldiers trained, the better off we'll be."

The minutes, as he was painfully aware, were ticking away all too rapidly. Where on the previous occasion the plant-creatures had seemed to grow with miraculous speed, now they hardly appeared to grow at all. What was that old motto again—a watched pot never boils? Motto proverb, whatever it was—and whatever a pot was—it expressed what was happening now. Watched plants never grew.

Somehow, however, they became full size, and then they began to free themselves from the soil. Newell switched on his flashlight and began to coordinate his light signals with spoken commands.

It was amazing to see how quickly they learned to obey—or rather, were conditioned to obey, for of learning in any conscious sense there could be none. Quickly he reached the point where he could march them back and forth across the field by the spoken word alone.

Up above him, the spaceship flashed again. Fortunately, it did not land nearby. Time, he was reminded, was growing short. It was almost with a sense of desperation that he went on with his military drill.

He had taught them to march and maneuver. Now he had to teach them to kill.

IT WAS NOT human beings that would be their enemies, not even Bulkley. Bulkley he would take care of himself. It was the other plant-creatures, their own kind. That's what soldiers are good for, he thought, to kill each other. They mustn't be too ambitious about killing their superiors. In the days when wars were common, there was a saying that generals died in bed.

But General Bulkley wouldn't die peacefully in bed, not if he could help it. For compared with Newell's army, Bulkley's would be at a disadvantage. Bulkley's soldiers had been taught to slaughter human beings, to locate their weak points and attack with a vicious fury that terrified the victims. Put them up against creatures of their own kind, and they'd strike for the heart or throat—and in plants such weak points simply didn't exist. Plants couldn't be terrified, either.

True, there were points of vulnerability in these plant-creatures as well—but Bulkley wasn't enough of a botanist to know exactly where they were. *But I do know,* Newell said to himself, *I'll teach my army. I'll teach them to paralyze the centers of motion in the branches that look and act like arms and legs, to cut off the vital metabolic impulses. When I'm through with them, they'll be perfect killers of their own kind.*

They learned rapidly. It was hardly more than an hour after he had begun this phase of their teaching when Indra suggested, "How will they know which ones to attack? In the actual battle, they might mistake each other for the enemy."

"Good idea. We'll have to give them, if not uniforms, at least distinguishing insignia. They can get green creepers from some of the forest trees, tie them around their arms."

Indra's father was watching the last-minute preparations—the final checkup before Newell set his amazing army into motion. "There is something vastly impressive about a display of military might," he said. "Would that human beings had as much discipline as these thoughtless vegetable creatures! I have often pondered, sir, that the chief weakness of the younger generation lies in its lack of discipline. Young people are unruly, disrespectful of their elders, intolerant of the accumulated wisdom and experience of those who have lived before them. They believe that wisdom begins with them. These plant-soldiers, on the other hand, respect authority and wisdom. They obey, immediately and implicitly."

Newell was not listening. His army was ready, to do or die. He, as the general, was now suffering the uncertainty of all leaders of armed men who have great decisions to make. He would have liked to give them further training, but time was growing short. Already he might have de-layed too long.

He flashed the green signal that meant, "Forward, march."

And his army began to march.

It was as if a forest had picked itself up, tree by tree, root and branch, and set itself into motion. A phrase from an old play in one of the extinct Earth languages sprang into his mind: "Till Birnam Wood do come to Dun-sinane." He remembered that to those old Earthmen the phrase had been a mere bit of trickery, a juggling with words. Now the words had acquired a literal and terrifying meaning.

The plant-soldiers moved forward slowly and inexorably. How long, Newell asked himself, until they reached the hut, the hut where Bulkley was lying in wait to slaughter the crew of the new ship?

An hour and a half at the quickest.

If Bulkley suspected anything, if he had been foresighted enough to spy on what Newell had been doing, he would surely try to stop the advancing army, burn them as Newell had done earlier. Newell realized he would have to watch out for traps, although he may not recognize them until too late—until after they were already sprung. And he had to hope that the ship didn't suddenly decide to land.

CHAPTER NINE

ONE, TWO, three, four, *one,* two, three, four. It was a grim burlesque of a human army, four thousand wooden feet marching to a single rhythm. *One,* two three, four, one, two, three, four—they keep going remorselessly, tirelessly. No sound of talk to break the rhythm of marching, no irregularities of step to betray the inhuman weakness.

It was hard for Newell breathe. He could feel the breath drying in his open mouth. He could sense the rapid beating of his heart. He felt a sudden pain—knots tying themselves in his stomach and writhing in the effort to get untied. Newell figured this was how it felt to go into battle in the old days, when the human race was still young and foolish. This was what it meant to march, under orders, into the jaws of death.

Newell's thoughts were racing again. *Bulkley is armed. Bulkley has weapons that can tear apart both human and plant bodies. Me, I have nothing but my own bare hands to fight with. The hypnotizer is useless now. It has no effect beyond a narrow radius, and there's a danger that it would hypnotize my own soldiers instead of Bulkley's. Can't take the chance of using it, can't risk it.*

One, two, three, four, one, two, three, four. Human soldiers don't need hypnotizers, the rhythm itself is hypnotic. Getting used to it. I'm breathing more normally now, my stomach hurts less, and my heart is beating more regularly. How long have we been marching? A quarter of an hour at most. But now the fear and uncertainty are gone, now I'm ready to face anything. I'm not ready yet to laugh at danger. But it's easier now to pretend that it doesn't exist.

What's that noise in back of me? Two people—funny. I was forgetting about people. All I was thinking of was my nonhuman army. Indra and her father, walking a short distance behind me, the old man giving his comments on the younger generation as usual, the girl white-faced and determined. She sees me turn, she's waving to me.

Maybe I'd better order her back, command her to stay out of danger. She wouldn't obey, though. And besides, perhaps it's better this way. If my army is victorious there'll be no danger. Bulkley doesn't want to shoot her, and my plant-soldiers will protect her from other enemies. That is, they'll protect her if all goes well, if they succeed in doing as I taught them. If they fail, if the battle goes against us, she'll probably die on the field. The thought of it scares me, but it's better, a lot better, than having her fall into Bulkley's hands.

One, two, three, four, *one*, two, three, four. Another quarter of an hour went by; a third of the distance had been covered and still no sign of the ship. Time was still in Newell's favor.

One, two, three, four, *one*, two, three—something happened to Newell's rhythm. A brown and white object rose from the ground and threw itself at his startled body. A wooden arm clutched for his throat; there was the feel of bark bruising his skin. Smart guy, Bulkley. Hit at the general, leave the army leaderless. Kill the general...

Newell's hands were on the wooden arm, trying desperately to wrench it away. His strength was against the strength of an unfeeling plant-creature's. His muscles of flesh and blood were straining against a wooden firmness. He was raining perspiration on his forehead. He and his attacker were soon deadlocked—neither of them able to move. Both were straining, motionless...

Then the deadlock was broken. Newell's own soldiers had remembered their lessons and applied the training he had given them, rallying to his support. The wooden arms of his enemy fall limply away; the brown and white form collapsing into a heap.

Good soldiers.

NEWELL'S army was slightly disorganized by the sudden attack, but quick light signals brought them to a halt. He signaled to reform ranks quickly, to march on again.

So Bulkley has scouts out to watch for me. I haven't given him too much credit. Bulkley is no fool. But the question still remains: has he taught his own soldiers a defense against the attack of their own kind?

Up above, a silvery light was flashing once more. This time the ship wasn't going away. The great shape was cruising back and forth, slowly, as if on guard. Then it seemed to grow larger.

Newell called back to Indra, "The ship's coming in for a landing! We'll be too late after all!"

"Not unless they lose all their sense of caution. They're not being reckless. Even after they land, they may not leave the ship until after they've done as much investigation as possible by instrument. If we could only get our own soldiers to move faster..."

"I don't see how, unless—wait a minute, I've got an idea. If I intensify the stimulus I may get a stronger response. I'll turn the green signal on as strong as possible, and keep it on."

He swept the green light across the field, back and forth, back and forth, but their was no response. That's what it seemed like at first, anyway. But after a time the army gradually picked up speed. The rhythm was quickening, quickening. Now it was *one*-and-two-and-*three*-and-four. Now they moved ahead at nearly twice their former speed.

But the ship was coming lower and lower. In another few minutes it would land.

Old man Hilton was protesting to the rear. Newell could hear him complaining that the quickened pace of the advance was leaving him behind.

Another twisted figure sprung at Newell, but this time he wasn't taken by surprise. This time he reacted quickly, dodging the dangerous wooden arms and leaving his soldiers to dispose of the intruder. Whatever else happened, he mustn't delay the main body of his troops.

The ship was easing down close to the ground. Someone aboard must have seen the other patrol ship, for the place of landing was little more than a hundred yards away from the previous wreck.

Newell's army was just ten minutes now—ten desperate minutes. *Let them stay inside for those ten minutes, and they'll be safe. If only I can warn them in some way…*

Have to run ahead, thread my way through my own soldiers. The rapid pace is telling on me now. Mouth and throat are both dry, and it's hard to breathe.

But that won't stop me. I'm in front of the men now, as a brave leader should be. A quarter of a mile away I can see an outer door of the spaceship tremble. They're going to come out.

"Stay in!" Newell didn't know he could yell that loud. "Don't come out! Danger!"

HAD THEY heard him? Had they picked up his warning on one of their instruments? Or had they been too careless to listen.

The door stayed shut.

Two figures sprang at him. He tried to twist aside, but other figures cut off his path, and still others blocked his retreat. For a moment they surrounded him, grim and impassive as death. Then his own soldiers reached him. The battle was joined.

The field was filled with forms that writhed as if under the blows of a hurricane. What seemed to Newell the most striking feature of the battle was that it was so quiet. Desperate duels were going on in a hundred different places; destruction lay in wait in a hundred different forms—and every one of them silent. These were soldiers that could neither utter shouts to terrify their opponents, nor cry out in pain. At most there was the occasional creak as of branches swaying in the wind, a sharp crack as of a tree trunk splitting in two. The whole scene, so quiet and so terrifying, had the quality of a painted nightmare.

A giant sword stroke seemed to slash through the battlefield, cutting across friend and foe alike. One of Bulkley's creatures had fired a real weapon. In the path of the deadly beam, a series of flames broke out. In a matter of moments, the battlefield was a blaze of fire.

Palls of smoke drifted over the weird struggling forms, making the nightmare even more horrible. A third of the soldiers originally on the field had already fallen, and it seemed to Newell that, among the slaughtered, most were Bulkley's. The training against human beings that the man had given his creatures had been fatally deficient against other creatures like themselves.

The doors of the ship had not opened. Now, Newell saw the guns swivel around and prepare to go into action. Apparently the patrol ship captain, unable to tell friend from foe, cared little which of the seemingly hostile creatures he slaughtered.

The purple signal of retreat flashed over the battlefield. Newell's soldiers drew back, leaving the open ground to the enemy.

A burst of heavy rays came from the ship and swept the field. Within five seconds, only a few scattered soldiers of Bulkley's army were left standing, and these were burning like torches. The battle was over.

The ship door slid open. Two men with a gun edged out cautiously, their nostrils wrinkling as they caught a whiff of the acrid smoke-filled air. Behind them came two others, similarly armed.

Newell came forward stiffly. He felt exhausted, as if by a day of hard work, although the sun seemed hardly to have moved in the sky. He realized with amazement that the entire slaughter had taken less than half an hour.

"Lift your hands," said one of the men sharply. "And come forward t'" be searched for weapons."

Newell would have smiled, if his facial muscles had not been so frozen. "I have no weapons. I'm the man who warned you."

"Where's the leader of these creatures?"

"Probably running for his life. He hoped to catch you by surprise, as he caught the other ship."

"What happened to them?"

CHAPTER TEN

NEWELL explained, as briefly as he could. Then he was brought into the ship, to explain all over again to the captain.

The latter frowned. "He's probably saved a few slaves."

"And he may be able to create more. The method isn't too difficult. And he may have found another vial of the chemical that I took from him. He's still dangerous."

"He'll have to be caught. You know his habits. And you know this section of the planet. Do you think you can lead us to him?"

"I'll try. We'll have to be wary, though. In forests like these, it's easy to walk into an ambush."

"Yes. It's even possible to be led into one. I wonder, Newell, just how trustworthy you really are."

"Still remembering that I'm supposed to be a criminal, are you? Mr. Hilton and his daughter should be able to testify to my character. They're the ones who were kidnapped from the freighter."

"And they're still alive? Good. Where are they?"

Where were they? They had been close behind him the last time he had looked—but that had been at least a half-hour ago, at the beginning of the battle. Newell felt the blood drain out of his face at the thought that they might have fallen into the desperate Bulkley's hands.

"I thought they were near me, Captain. They must have become lost during the battle."

"You don't think they might have been taken prisoner by Bulkley, do you?" demanded the Captain sharply.

"I'm afraid so, sir."

"That's another reason for finding him in a hurry. Newell, you may have a couple of my men, with a heavy gun. I can't spare any more."

"I won't need any more, sir. I have my own plant-soldiers. They're trained to attack others of their kind, but not human beings. They'll take care of the creatures that Bulkley still has left, and make it possible for us to get at him."

The fatigue of a moment ago was gone. Now fear for Indra and her father seemed to race through his blood, arousing him to new and greater efforts.

Where could Bulkley have taken them? Not across the field, not under the guns of the ship. He must have drawn back from the plastex hut, first stripping it of the things he thought he would need most. Chemicals to create new dragon-tooth seeds, tubes to create light—a generator unit. He would not let go of these if he could help it.

The two men the Captain had assigned to him were waiting. "Stay with me," he ordered. To his plant-soldiers he flashed a light signal. "Deploy across the field, then advance."

They spread out and moved forward. Smoke drifted across the sky from the still smoldering battlefield, but here, where no fighting had taken place, the ground itself was redolent of leaves and grasses, of small creepers and flowering shrubs.

Now we'll see, thought Newell, *which general will die in bed and which with his boots on. This time it's the showdown—either Bulkley or me. But he has a powerful threat in what he can do to Indra and her father.*

Everything looks peaceful now, no sign of danger anywhere. Wonder how many slaves Bulkley has left. Less than a score out of the two thousand he started with, the two thousand I gave him. They won't help him now. And neither will his weapons. I'll tear him apart with my bare hands if I have to.

THE WOODEN army came to a sudden confused halt. Before them stood a man—Hilton himself, holding up his hand in warning. Newell exclaimed, "Mr. Hilton? You're safe! But where's Indra?"

"That, sir, is what I am about to explain to you. Do not advance, Mr. Newell. And tell your men, if I may be permitted to employ the expression to refer to such obviously nonhuman creatures, to remain in position. I am here, sir, under duress. I am, despite what you conceive to be my freedom to speak to you, a captive."

"Then Bulkley's in back of you, holding a gun on you...?"

"You surmise the situation correctly, Mr. Newell, and state it concisely. In order to complete the picture, however, I must add that my daughter..." His resonant voice faltered for a moment, then picked up again. "...my daughter is also being threatened with death."

"It won't help him. Do you hear that, Bulkley, wherever you are? Your goose is cooked now. Your only chance is to surrender and plead for mercy."

There was a moment's silence. Then the old man said, "He will not answer directly, for fear of revealing his position. He is within earshot, but I myself cannot state precisely where."

"That won't help him either."

"I devoutly hope not, Mr. Newell, but I must none the less repeat the message he gave me. Either you surrender, or my own life and my daughter's will be forfeit. I am not intimidated, sir, although if not for this unfortunate occurrence. I should still have many years of useful existence before me. I am in my vigorous one hundred and twenties, and my father, as you may not know, lived more than forty years beyond that age, until an unhappy accident…"

Newell lost track of the old man's wandering words. He remembered only that he had to save Indra. Somewhere near them, Bulkley was hiding, the girl probably gagged to keep her from crying out. And she was probably being held by one of Bulkley's few remaining slaves, so that she couldn't run away. But where was the group concealed?

He caught the thread of the old man's words. "And those, sir, are his terms."

"Say that again!"

"I thought I had made the conditions clear. Nevertheless, sir, I shall repeat. Mr. Bulkley asks you to throw down your weapons and come forward unarmed—after giving orders to you men to retreat."

"He wants me to put myself in his power, is that it?"

"That is the situation, Mr. Newell. Otherwise he will murder my daughter and me."

Newell shouted, "I have no weapons with me, Bulkley, so I can't throw them down. But that won't stop me from coming at you."

"Wait, Mr. Newell. First you must order your men to retreat."

"I'll signal them, all right."

He put his hand in his pocket and drew out the hypnotizer. The light began to glow, to go through its pulsing sequence of colors.

His own plant-creatures stood as if paralyzed. And Bulkley's? They must see it too. Whichever ones were holding Indra could no longer exert their strength. If she sensed their lack of power, and wrenched herself free...

There was a sudden creaking as of branches swaying from twenty-five yards ahead of them, an abrupt curse of anger and desperation. A small black object suddenly shot into the air—Bulkley's gun. Newell raced toward the scene of struggle, covering the ground in a dozen strides.

At one side stood Indra, wrenching at the gag on her mouth, her face scratched, her hair disheveled. Near her was Bulkley, struggling in the grip of a pair of his own creatures. The brown and white caricatures of faces were familiar. In the fraction of a second that it took Newell to grasp the scene, he recognized the features of the pair he had called Tough-Egg and Scar-Face.

ONE LAST choking cry came from Bulkley, and then there was a snap. His head fell forward, his body dropped to the ground.

The creatures that had killed, turned to run. Newell flashed a quick signal to his own followers, and seconds later the killers were surrounded and their wooden bodies taken apart.

Indra was in his arms. He held her tight, disregarding the two men the Captain had sent along with him. Finally he turned to them. "Thanks for your offer to be of help, gentlemen, but I have no further need of you."

One of them grinned. "I can see that."

"You can report to the Captain. Both of you."

They started on their way back. Indra shuddered in his arms. "Toward the end Bulkley was out of his mind, completely beyond control. He blamed you for upsetting all his plans. He wanted nothing but to kill you."

"He did his best."

"I tried to think of a way to stop him, but I was helpless. Then, when you started the hypnotizer going, I remembered what you had told me of its previous effect on these creatures, and was able to wrench myself free. Bulkley tried to turn the gun on me, but he was too close, and I was able to disarm him, using another jiu jitsu method. He rushed me when he realized I was getting away, and then I threw him over my head, and he landed on the creatures nearby. That's what set them off and made them turn on him."

"All those creatures he taught to kill human beings are dangerous. They'll have to be destroyed."

"Yes, I know. But they seem so human. It will be like murder."

"It won't be. They feel nothing." He went on slowly, "That may change, of course. As they learn more and more, they may develop some kind of genuine consciousness of the world around them. They may develop feelings. And then they'll offer a real problem."

"The ones you trained aren't harmful to us. And they could be useful."

"That's why I first invented them. To be useful. I thought I could show them to the authorities, prove I was capable of doing good work, and win back my rights as a citizen. This planet is dangerous to human beings. But plants can live here, and so could creatures descended from plants. They could build it up, make the planet part of an intergalactic system."

She nodded. "You're right."

"I think that when I explain all that, and the authorities realize what I've done here, and how Bulkley has tried to turn my work to vicious purposes, I'll have no trouble in getting them to reopen the original case, and convince them of my innocence of crime."

"And my father and I can continue with the vacation that Bulkley interrupted."

"Your father is getting too old to travel. You need another companion. And it won't be a vacation. It'll be more like a honeymoon. In fact, it will be one."

It was at that moment that a sonorous voice came to them. "I have been cogitating, Mr. Newell, and my meditations concern the ethical and sociological aspects of the problems involved in the existence of these plant-creatures. Recalling the many experiences with strange and unexpected forms of life on many galaxies..."

Newell bit back an expression of extreme annoyance. Indra said sweetly "Father! "Look at this, Father..."

She held up the hypnotizer that the old man himself had constructed. The light began to glow and pulse.

A glazed look came into the eyes of the man whom millions of listeners and viewers knew as Dr. Hypno. The facial muscles relaxed, the eyes stared blankly.

"He hasn't the slightest idea of what's going on in front of his nose," said Indra demurely.

Which was a good thing, thought Newell, as he stretched out his hungry arms.

THE END

If you've enjoyed this book, you will not want to miss these terrific titles...

ARMCHAIR SCI-FI & HORROR DOUBLE NOVELS, $12.95 each

D-51   **A GOD NAMED SMITH** by Henry Slesar
WORLDS OF THE IMPERIUM by Keith Laumer

D-52   **CRAIG'S BOOK** by Don Wilcox
EDGE OF THE KNIFE by H. Beam Piper

D-53   **THE SHINING CITY** by Rena M. Vale
THE RED PLANET by Russ Winterbotham

D-54   **THE MAN WHO LIVED TWICE** by Rog Phillips
VALLEY OF THE CROEN by Lee Tarbell

D-55   **OPERATION DISASTER** by Milton Lesser
LAND OF THE DAMNED by Berkeley Livingston

D-56   **CAPTIVE OF THE CENTAURIANESS** by Poul Anderson
A PRINCESS OF MARS by Edgar Rice Burroughs

D-57   **THE NON-STATISTICAL MAN** by Raymond F. Jones
MISSION FROM MARS by Rick Conroy

D-58   **INTRUDERS FROM THE STARS** by Ross Rocklynne
FLIGHT OF THE STARLING by Chester S. Geier

D-59   **COSMIC SABOTEUR** by Frank M. Robinson
LOOK TO THE STARS by Willard Hawkins

D-60   **THE MOON IS HELL!** by John W. Campbell, Jr.
THE GREEN WORLD by Hal Clement

ARMCHAIR SCIENCE FICTION CLASSICS, $12.95 each

C-16   **THE SHAVER MYSTERY, Book Three**
by Richard S. Shaver

C-17   **THE PLANET STRAPPERS**
by Raymond Z. Gallun

C-18   **THE FOURTH "R"**
by George O. Smith

ARMCHAIR SCI-FI & HORROR GEMS SERIES, $12.95 each

G-5   **SCIENCE FICTION GEMS, Vol. Three**
C. M. Kornbluth and others

G-6   **HORROR GEMS, Vol. Three**
August Derleth and others

If you've enjoyed this book, you will not want to miss these terrific titles...

ARMCHAIR SCI-FI & HORROR DOUBLE NOVELS, $12.95 each

D-61 **THE MAN WHO STOPPED AT NOTHING** by Paul W. Fairman
TEN FROM INFINITY by Ivar Jorgensen

D-62 **WORLDS WITHIN** by Rog Phillips
THE SLAVE by C.M. Kornbluth

D-63 **SECRET OF THE BLACK PLANET** by Milton Lesser
THE OUTCASTS OF SOLAR III by Emmett McDowell

D-64 **WEB OF THE WORLDS** by Harry Harrison and Katherine MacLean
RULE GOLDEN by Damon Knight

D-65 **TEN TO THE STARS** by Raymond Z. Gallun
THE CONQUERORS by David H. Keller, M. D.

D-66 **THE HORDE FROM INFINITY** by Dwight V. Swain
THE DAY THE EARTH FROZE by Gerald Hatch

D-67 **THE WAR OF THE WORLDS** by H. G. Wells
THE TIME MACHINE by H. G. Wells

D-68 **STARCOMBERS** by Edmond Hamilton
THE YEAR WHEN STARDUST FELL by Raymond F. Jones

D-69 **HOCUS-POCUS UNIVERSE** by Jack Williamson
QUEEN OF THE PANTHER WORLD by Berkeley Livingston

D-70 **BATTERING RAMS OF SPACE** by Don Wilcox
DOOMSDAY WING by George H. Smith

ARMCHAIR SCIENCE FICTION CLASSICS, $12.95 each

C-19 **EMPIRE OF JEGGA**
by David V. Reed

C-20 **THE TOMORROW PEOPLE**
by Judith Merril

C-21 **THE MAN FROM YESTERDAY**
by Howard Browne as by Lee Francis

C-22 **THE TIME TRADERS**
by Andre Norton

C-23 **ISLANDS OF SPACE**
by John W. Campbell

C-24 **THE GALAXY PRIMES**
by E. E. "Doc" Smith

If you've enjoyed this book, you will not want to miss these terrific titles…

ARMCHAIR SCI-FI & HORROR DOUBLE NOVELS, $12.95 each

D-71 **THE DEEP END** by Gregory Luce
 TO WATCH BY NIGHT by Robert Moore Williams

D-72 **SWORDSMAN OF LOST TERRA** by Poul Anderson
 PLANET OF GHOSTS by David V. Reed

D-73 **MOON OF BATTLE** by J. J. Allerton
 THE MUTANT WEAPON by Murray Leinster

D-74 **OLD SPACEMEN NEVER DIE!** John Jakes
 RETURN TO EARTH by Bryan Berry

D-75 **THE THING FROM UNDERNEATH** by Milton Lesser
 OPERATION INTERSTELLAR by George O. Smith

D-76 **THE BURNING WORLD** by Algis Budrys
 FOREVER IS TOO LONG by Chester S. Geier

D-77 **THE COSMIC JUNKMAN** by Rog Phillips
 THE ULTIMATE WEAPON by John W. Campbell

D-78 **THE TIES OF EARTH** by James H. Schmitz
 CUE FOR QUIET by Thomas L. Sherred

D-79 **SECRET OF THE MARTIANS** by Paul W. Fairman
 THE VARIABLE MAN by Philip K. Dick

D-80 **THE GREEN GIRL** by Jack Williamson
 THE ROBOT PERIL by Don Wilcox

ARMCHAIR SCIENCE FICTION CLASSICS, $12.95 each

C-25 **THE STAR KINGS**
 by Edmond Hamilton

C-26 **NOT IN SOLITUDE**
 by Kenneth Gantz

C-32 **PROMETHEUS II**
 by S. J. Byrne

ARMCHAIR SCI-FI & HORROR GEMS SERIES, $12.95 each

G-7 **SCIENCE FICTION GEMS, Vol. Four**
 Jack Sharkey and others

G-8 **HORROR GEMS, Vol. Four**
 Seabury Quinn and others

If you've enjoyed this book, you will not want to miss these terrific titles…

ARMCHAIR SCI-FI & HORROR DOUBLE NOVELS, $12.95 each

D-81   **THE LAST PLEA** by Robert Bloch
THE STATUS CIVILIZATION by Robert Sheckley

D-82   **WOMAN FROM ANOTHER PLANET** by Frank Belknap Long
HOMECALLING by Judith Merril

D-83   **WHEN TWO WORLDS MEET** by Robert Moore Williams
THE MAN WHO HAD NO BRAINS by Jeff Sutton

D-84   **THE SPECTRE OF SUICIDE SWAMP** by E. K. Jarvis
IT'S MAGIC, YOU DOPE! by Jack Sharkey

D-85   **THE STARSHIP FROM SIRIUS** by Rog Phillips
FINAL WEAPON by Everett Cole

D-86   **TREASURE ON THUNDER MOON** by Edmond Hamilton
TRAIL OF THE ASTROGAR by Henry Haase

D-87   **THE VENUS ENIGMA** by Joe Gibson
THE WOMAN IN SKIN 13 by Paul W. Fairman

D-88   **THE MAD ROBOT** by William P. McGivern
THE RUNNING MAN by J. Holly Hunter

D-89   **VENGEANCE OF KYVOR** by Randall Garrett
AT THE EARTH'S CORE by Edgar Rice Burroughs

D-90   **DWELLERS OF THE DEEP** by Don Wilcox
NIGHT OF THE LONG KNIVES by Fritz Leiber

ARMCHAIR SCIENCE FICTION CLASSICS, $12.95 each

C-28   **THE MAN FROM TOMORROW**
by Stanton A. Coblentz

C-29   **THE GREEN MAN OF GRAYPEC**
by Festus Pragnell

C-30   **THE SHAVER MYSTERY, Book Four**
by Richard S. Shaver

ARMCHAIR MASTERS OF SCIENCE FICTION SERIES, $16.95 each

MS-7   **MASTERS OF SCIENCE FICTION AND FANTASY, Vol. Seven**
Lester del Rey, "The Band Played On" and other tales

MS-8   **MASTERS OF SCIENCE FICTION, Vol. Eight**
Milton Lesser, "'A' as in Android" and other tales

If you've enjoyed this book, you will not want to miss these terrific titles…

ARMCHAIR SCI-FI & HORROR DOUBLE NOVELS, $12.95 each

D-91   **THE TIME TRAP** by Henry Kuttner
        THE LUNAR LICHEN by Hal Clement

D-92   **SARGASSO OF LOST STARSHIPS** by Poul Anderson
        THE ICE QUEEN by Don Wilcox

D-93   **THE PRINCE OF SPACE** by Jack Williamson
        POWER by Harl Vincent

D-94   **PLANET OF NO RETURN** by Howard Browne
        THE ANNIHILATOR COMES by Ed Earl Repp

D-95   **THE SINISTER INVASION** by Edmond Hamilton
        OPERATION TERROR by Murray Leinster

D-96   **TRANSIENT** by Ward Moore
        THE WORLD-MOVER by George O. Smith

D-97   **FORTY DAYS HAS SEPTEMBER** by Milton Lesser
        THE DEVIL'S PLANET by David Wright O'Brien

D-98   **THE CYBERENE** by Rog Phillips
        BADGE OF INFAMY by Lester del Rey

D-99   **THE JUSTICE OF MARTIN BRAND** by Raymond A. Palmer
        BRING BACK MY BRAIN by Dwight V. Swain

D-100   **WIDE-OPEN PLANET** by L. Sprague de Camp
        AND THEN THE TOWN TOOK OFF by Richard Wilson

ARMCHAIR SCIENCE FICTION CLASSICS, $12.95 each

C-31   **THE GOLDEN GUARDSMEN**
        by S. J. Byrne

C-32   **ONE AGAINST THE MOON**
        by Donald A. Wollheim

C-33   **HIDDEN CITY**
        by Chester S. Geier

ARMCHAIR SCI-FI & HORROR GEMS SERIES, $12.95 each

G-9   **SCIENCE FICTION GEMS, Vol. Five**
        Clifford D. Simak and others

G-10   **HORROR GEMS, Vol. Five**
        E. Hoffman Price and others

If you've enjoyed this book, you will not want to miss these terrific titles...

ARMCHAIR SCI-FI & HORROR DOUBLE NOVELS, $12.95 each

D-101 **THE CONQUEST OF THE PLANETS** by John W. Campbell
THE MAN WHO ANNEXED THE MOON by Bob Olsen

D-102 **WEAPON FROM THE STARS** by Rog Phillips
THE EARTH WAR by Mack Reynolds

D-103 **THE ALIEN INTELLIGENCE** by Jack Williamson
INTO THE FOURTH DIMENSION by Ray Cummings

D-104 **THE CRYSTAL PLANETOIDS** by Stanton A. Coblentz
SURVIVORS FROM 9,000 B. C. by Robert Moore Williams

D-105 **THE TIME PROJECTOR** by David H. Keller, M.D. and David Lasser
STRANGE COMPULSION by Philip Jose Farmer

D-106 **WHOM THE GODS WOULD SLAY** by Paul W. Fairman
MEN IN THE WALLS by William Tenn

D-107 **LOCKED WORLDS** by Edmond Hamilton
THE LAND THAT TIME FORGOT by Edgar Rice Burroughs

D-108 **STAY OUT OF SPACE** by Dwight V. Swain
REBELS OF THE RED PLANET by Charles L. Fontenay

D-109 **THE METAMORPHS** by S. J. Byrne
MICROCOSMIC BUCCANEERS by Harl Vincent

D-110 **YOU CAN'T ESCAPE FROM MARS** by E. K. Jarvis
THE MAN WITH FIVE LIVES by David V. Reed

ARMCHAIR SCIENCE FICTION CLASSICS, $12.95 each

C-34 **30 DAY WONDER**
by Richard Wilson

C-35 **G.O.G. 666**
by John Taine

C-36 **RALPH 124C 41+**
by Hugo Gernsback

ARMCHAIR SCI-FI & HORROR GEMS SERIES, $12.95 each

G-11 **SCIENCE FICTION GEMS, Vol. Six**
Edmond Hamilton and others

G-12 **HORROR GEMS, Vol. Six**
H. P. Lovecraft and others

If you've enjoyed this book, you will not want to miss these terrific titles...

ARMCHAIR SCI-FI & HORROR DOUBLE NOVELS, $12.95 each

D-111 **THE MOON ERA** by Jack Williamson
REVENGE OF THE ROBOTS by Howard Browne

D-112 **SON OF THE BLACK CHALICE** by Milton Lesser
SENTRY OF THE SKY by Evelyn E. Smith

D-113 **OUTPOST ON THE MOON** by Joslyn Maxwell
POTENTIAL ZERO by S. J. Byrne

D-114 **OUTPOST INFINITY** by Raymond F. Jones
THE WHITE INVADERS by Ray Cummings

D-115 **TIME TRAP** by Rog Phillips
THE COSMIC DESTROYER by Alexander Blade

D-116 **THE OTHER SIDE OF THE MOON** by Edmond Hamilton
SECRET INVASION by Walter Kubilius

D-117 **DANGER MOON** by Frederik Pohl
THE HIDDEN UNIVERSE by Ralph Milne Farley

D-118 **THE WAILING ASTEROID** by Murray Leinster
THE WORLD THAT COULDN'T BE by Clifford D. Simak

D-119 **THE WHISPERING GORILLA** by Don Wilcox
RETURN OF THE WHISPERING GORILLA by David V. Reed

D-120 **SPECIAL EFFECT** by J. F. Bone
WARLORD OF KOR by Terry Carr

ARMCHAIR SCIENCE FICTION CLASSICS, $12.95 each

C-37 **THE GREEN MAN RETURNS**
by Harold M. Sherman

C-38 **THE SHAVER MYSTERY, Book Five**
by Richard S, Shaver

C-39 **MARS CHILD**
by Cyril Judd

ARMCHAIR MASTERS OF SCIENCE FICTION SERIES, $16.95 each

MS-9 **MASTERS OF SCIENCE FICTION AND FANTASY, Vol. Nine**
Poul Anderson, "The Star Beast" and other tales

MS-10 **MASTERS OF SCIENCE FICTION, Vol. Ten**
Robert Moore Williams, "Time Tolls for Toro" and other tales

If you've enjoyed this book, you will not want to miss these terrific titles…

www.ingramcontent.com/pod-product-compliance
Lightning Source LLC
Chambersburg PA
CBHW030318180626
46810CB00003B/1138